THE PUBLIC IMAGE

MURIEL SPARK DBE, CLit, FRSE, FRSL was born in Edinburgh in 1918. A poet, essayist, biographer and novelist, she won much international praise, receiving the James Tait Black Memorial Prize in 1965 for *The Mandelbaum Gate*, the US Ingersoll Foundation TS Eliot Award in 1992 and the David Cohen Prize in 1997. She was twice shortlisted for the Booker Prize (for *The Public Image* in 1969 and *Loitering with Intent* in 1981) and, in 2010, was shortlisted for the 'Lost Man Booker Prize' of 1970. In 1993 Muriel Spark was made a Dame for services to literature. In 1998 she was awarded the Golden PEN Award for a 'Lifetime's Distinguished Service to Literature'. She died in Tuscany in 2006.

LUCY ELLMANN is an American-born writer, now living in Edinburgh. Her first novel, *Sweet Desserts*, won the Guardian Fiction Prize. As a literary critic, she has contributed to *The New York Times*, the *Independent*, the *Guardian*, the *Times Literary Supplement*, the *Spectator*, the *New Statesman* and other publications. Her most recent novel is *Mimi*.

Novels by Muriel Spark in Polygon

The Comforters
Robinson
Memento Mori
The Ballad of Peckham Rye
The Bachelors
The Prime of Miss Jean Brodie
The Girls of Slender Means
The Mandelbaum Gate
The Public Image
The Driver's Seat
Not to Disturb
The Hothouse by the East River
The Abbess of Crewe
The Takeover
Territorial Rights
Loitering with Intent
The Only Problem
A Far Cry from Kensington
Symposium
Reality and Dreams
Aiding and Abetting
The Finishing School

THE PUBLIC IMAGE

Muriel Spark

Introduced by Lucy Ellmann

FT

This edition published in Great Britain in 2018
by Polygon, an imprint of Birlinn Ltd.

Birlinn Ltd
West Newington House
10 Newington Road
Edinburgh
EH9 1QS

www.polygonbooks.co.uk

1

ISBN 978 1 84697 433 5

The publisher gratefully acknowledges investment from
Creative Scotland towards the publication of this book.

Supported by the Muriel Spark Society

British Library Cataloguing-in-Publication Data
A catalogue record for this book is available
on request from the British Library.

Typeset by Biblichor Ltd, Edinburgh
Printed and bound in Malta by Gutenberg Press

Foreword

Muriel Spark was born in Edinburgh on the first of February, 1918. She was the second child of Cissy and Bernard Camberg, an engineer from a family of Jewish and Lithuanian extraction. Her early life is recalled in loving and meticulous detail in her autobiography, *Curriculum Vitae*, published in 1992. Hers was a working-class upbringing, but while money was tight she was in no way deprived. Her mother was gregarious and extrovert, always singing songs and telling stories, and wearing the kind of clothes that made her unmissable among other, more dully dressed women in the Bruntsfield neighbourhood.

When she was five years old Spark began her education at James Gillespie's High School for Girls where she remained until she was sixteen. It was a period she remembered with great fondness. She was anointed the school's 'Poet and Dreamer' and many of her early verses appeared in its magazine. In 1929, she first encountered an inspirational teacher, a spinster called Christina Kay, who was to have a formative effect on her life. It was Miss Kay, for example, who took her and her friends – 'the crème de la crème' – on long walks through the city's Old Town, to exhibitions, concerts and poetry readings, and who insisted that she must become a writer. 'I felt I had hardly much choice in the matter,' Spark wrote later. In her sixth and most famous novel, *The Prime of Miss Jean Brodie*, the main character was modelled closely, if not actually, on Miss Kay. Like the unorthodox Miss Brodie, Miss Kay was an Italophile and a naive admirer of Mussolini, of whom she pinned a picture on a wall together with paintings by Renaissance masters.

On leaving school Spark enrolled in a course for précis-writing at Heriot-Watt College. She then found a job as secretary to the owner of a department store in Princes Street, the Scottish capital's main thoroughfare. At a dance she met Sydney Oswald Spark, a lapsed Jew, whose initials she felt in hindsight should have warned her to steer clear of him. Like her father's parents, 'SOS' had been born in Lithuania. She was nineteen, he was thirty-two. He planned to teach in Africa, and Muriel, eager to leave Edinburgh and launch herself at life, agreed to become engaged. In August 1937, she followed him to Southern Rhodesia (now Zimbabwe) and the following month they were married. Their son, Robin, was born in 1938. Soon thereafter the couple separated.

The outbreak of war the following year meant Spark could not return home as she had hoped and she had no option but to stay in Africa. In 1944, however, she obtained a divorce and returned to Britain on a troop ship. Having settled her son with her parents, she headed for London where the devastation of the Blitz was everywhere evident. She boarded at the Helena Club, the original of the May of Teck Club in *The Girls of Slender Means*, and found work in the Political Intelligence department of the Foreign Office, whose *raison d'être* was to disseminate anti-Nazi propaganda among the German population.

In the years immediately after the war she attempted to make a living as a writer. In 1947, she was appointed General Secretary of the Poetry Society and editor of its magazine, *Poetry Review*, but she fell foul of traditionalists, including Marie Stopes, a pioneer of birth control. It was a pity, Spark remarked, 'that her mother rather than she had not thought of birth control'. Her first book, *A Tribute to Wordsworth*, was co-written with her then lover, Derek Stanford, and published in 1950. A year later she won a short story competition in the *Observer* newspaper with 'The Seraph and the Zambesi'. In 1952, she published her debut collection of poetry, *The Fanfarlo and Other Verse*.

Her conversion to Catholicism in 1954 coincided with her beginning work on her first novel, *The Comforters*, which finally appeared in 1957. Praised by Graham Greene and Evelyn Waugh among others, it allowed Spark to give up part-time secretarial work and devote herself to writing. Four more novels – *Robinson*, *Memento Mori*, *The Ballad of Peckham Rye* and *The Bachelors*, and a collection of stories, *The Go-Away Bird* – followed in quick succession and enhanced her reputation for originality and wit.

It was with the publication in 1961 of *The Prime of Miss Jean Brodie*, however, that Spark became an international bestseller. It was turned into a play and a film for which Maggie Smith, who played the eponymous teacher, won the Oscar for Best Actress. Indeed, remarked Spark, so closely did Smith become associated with the part that many readers seemed to assume that she was her creator. The novel, which Spark liked to refer to as her 'milch cow', was a critical as well as a commercial success and continued to sell well throughout its author's long career. In America, it was first published in the *New Yorker*. Its editor, William Shawn, gave Spark an office in which to work. There, she wrote her next two novels, *The Girls of Slender Means* and *The Mandelbaum Gate*, which was awarded the James Tait Black Memorial Prize.

In 1967, having grown tired of the clamour and claustrophobia of life in New York, she moved to Italy and Rome.

That same year she was made an OBE. It also saw the publication of her first collected volumes of stories and poems. Novels continued to appear at regular intervals. *The Public Image* appeared in 1968 and was shortlisted for the Booker Prize. *The Driver's Seat*, which Spark believed to be her best, was published in 1970. In 1974 came *The Abbess of Crewe*, an inspired satire of the Watergate scandal, which she set in a convent.

In the mid 1970s Spark left Rome for Tuscany, settling in a rambling and venerable house deep in the countryside, owned by her friend, Penelope Jardine, an artist. Surrounded by fields of vines and olives, she was able to work without fear of interruption. *The Takeover*, *Territorial Rights* and *Loitering with Intent* – also shortlisted for the Booker – were among the first novels she wrote in the place that would be her final home. Among the many awards she received were the Ingersoll Foundation TS Eliot Award, the Scottish Arts Council Award for *Reality and Dreams*, the Boccaccio Prize for European Literature, the David Cohen British Literature Prize for a lifetime's achievement, and the Golden PEN Award from PEN International. In 1993, she was made a Dame.

Though in her later years she was often beset by illness, she never stopped writing. It was her calling and she pursued it with unfailing dedication. She always had a poem 'on the go' and she never wanted for ideas for novels and stories and plays. Among her later novels were *A Far Cry from Kensington*, *Symposium*, *Reality and Dreams* and *Aiding and Abetting*. Her valedictory novel was *The Finishing School*, the majority of whose characters are would-be writers, which was published in 2004. Spark died two years later at the age of eighty-eight and is buried in the walled cemetery of the village of Oliveto in the Val di Chiana. On her headstone, she is described in Italian with one simple word: *poeta*.

Introduction

Lucy Ellmann

It's hard to care about starlets. The #MeToo movement has shown not just how ready movie moguls are to take their trousers off during meetings, but the amount of personal and professional torment an actress must go through before we, the public, feel even an ounce of sympathy for her. The thing is, since the early days of cinema, peaking perhaps in the 1950s and 1960s, we've had so many movie stars thrown at us for our gladiatorial amusement, our thumbs up and thumbs down, that most of them just don't seem real. I often find myself wondering if they ever do any hoovering or washing-up. If you prick them, do they bleed? 'The actresses can make themselves cry,' says a penetrating child in *The Public Image*. As Muriel Spark notes in this wild bronco ride of a novel, stars adopt a certain remoteness, in return for all those close-ups on screen. It's the job of PR experts to make the dichotomy appear logical. They manufacture myths of bliss and simplicity which we lap up, tired of hearing how complicated human beings are. It's the novelist's job to dig deeper.

Annabel Christopher, an English actress of the 1960s, is described to us by everybody: her husband, their friends, neighbours, directors, film buffs, reporters and, repeatedly, by Spark herself, who circles ever closer to her prey. As a result of all these perspectives, you begin to get a sense of a personality at odds with, if not overwhelmed by, the projections of others. Annabel twists and turns in the eye of the beholder. But isn't that what an actor's for? Spark observes her with a cool and critical eye, calling her 'a puny little thing', and more than once suggests the actress has been accidentally exalted through no discernible merit of her own.

After the usual grim start in the UK, which hosts the dreariest film industry in the world, Annabel hits the jackpot and starts picking up roles in Hollywood and Rome. By chance, an eager Italian director fastens on her, declaring her eyes tigerish. From there, it's a small step to being named (by him) the 'English Lady-Tiger'. The idea spreads across the globe that, though prim and phlegmatic in public, Annabel's dynamite in bed. The belief is extended by Italian fan mags to explain British marital fidelity in general: 'these English tigresses knew how to hold their husbands'. Sex is so good, the theory goes, when you're married to a *tigress*, that Englishmen don't need to stray. This has to be one of the weirdest theories of British sexuality ever invented (asexuality being the more likely spur to Anglo–Saxon monogamy), and surely of wholly Sparkian origin. The true picture of Annabel's life is much less sensational: she's not all that reserved in person, and not great in bed. She likes to have sex once a week, in the dark, wearing a nightie and never upside down. 'I know it's kinky, but that's how I like it.'

Spark doesn't ignore the difficulties involved in getting us to care about this characterless movie star. While she exults in her vapidity, she also adroitly circumvents it by making Annabel real. First of all, she gives her a baby to look after, Carl, and right from the outset Annabel proves herself a conscientious, no-nonsense mother. When at home, she feeds and changes him regularly. 'She boiled his egg, two minutes.' When out, she calls home every three hours without fail, to see how he is. And he's fine – Carl's the little imperturbable king of this book, and just gets on with baby-hood. His bed is a *pillow*, a nice touch. Using a pillow case as a makeshift infant sleeping-bag seems a great idea, almost as appealing as putting a baby in a drawer. Mothers need short-cuts (though, in this instance, the strategy is not brought on by poverty or necessity, but simply stardom – Annabel's too busy, in the middle of memorising a script and moving into a fabulous but minimally furnished apartment in a palazzo, to provide Carl with a cot). Spark is always quick with the handy hints, like her own personal credo, 'When in doubt, go to Paris'. Another tip offered here: never make too many excuses at a time. 'More than one sounds false.' And, while you're at it, 'Avoid psychiatrists'.

To endear Annabel to us yet further, Spark gives her a traitorous quibbler of a husband who's always correcting Annabel's grammar. Frederick and his awful friend Billy, a grocer-boy turned film critic who can't seem to touch a piece of paper without leaving butter stains on it, routinely mock Annabel for her views, her looks, her intellect (or lack thereof) and aspirations, while contentedly availing them-selves of her vast income. Like two little Harvey Weinsteins, they slob around all day getting high on their own power and misogynistic inklings. 'Every few weeks he wanted to leave Annabel,' writes Spark of Frederick's growing antipathy.

He once wanted to be an actor, but would only consider 'substantial' roles (though *not* Shakespeare, for reasons mercifully left undisturbed). His aesthetic scruples are beside the point anyway, since he's never offered any acting jobs at all. He turns instead to writing screenplays, appar-ently producing far from original work that is nonetheless enough of a success (mostly because he sells his scripts cheap) to make it possible for him to play an important, if reluctant, part in the promotion of Annabel. With the help of the talented publicist Francesca, whom Frederick would happily bed, and her carefully crafted photographs and press releases, he and Annabel become a glamorous, triumphant duo, *à la* Posh and Becks. They are the objects of envy and frenzied desire, ready to take the world by storm, yet skating on thin ice.

A helpless egotist, Frederick proudly removes his name from movie credits when he feels his script's been mangled by the finished product, then quietly reinstates it when the movie starts to do well. Spark seems to find it hard to take movies seriously at all, deliciously summing up the absurdity of the parts Annabel plays early in her career: 'the typist who just happened to return to the office for the parcel she had forgotten when the fatal argument was in progress in the boss's room next door, the little housemaid whose unforeseen amorous exchanges with the delivery boy waylaid the flight plans of the kidnappers, the waif on the underground railway who was one of those who never got home to her lodgings . . .' A nice microcosm of male imaginings. Later on, in Frederick's own film (derivative, we gather, of *The Turn of the Screw*), Annabel plays a governess who ridiculously takes a dip in the Bernini fountain in the Piazza Navona, 'to cool off the passion she had conceived for the master of the house'. Every actress in the 1960s had to dunk herself in a Roman fountain. It must have been written into their contracts.

Meanwhile, Frederick and Billy continue their vilification campaign, mocking Annabel for any sign of pride in her 'public image'. But it's a *good* image, she feels. She's pretty happy with it. Frederick decides that 'nobody but he could know how shallow she really was. I know her, he thought, inside out. They don't.' There is a battle of the sexes going on here, over who earns the money and who deserves respect. Frederick longs for Francesca, with her 'old-rooted deference to men; she even gave a kind of instinctive precedence to a male cat over a female cat'. Casual infidelity ensues, on both sides: Frederick has his 'love-visits' to a humble girl in the suburbs, Annabel to an American drama student who doesn't like being laughed at. None of this defuses Frederick's gripes. When Annabel tells him about her professional troubles, he accuses her of treating him like a 'letter-box, a solid bright red pillar-box to post her letters in'. No wonder she's confused.

The question hovers over the novel: *is* Annabel stupid? Her husband thinks so, her directors hope so. Spark takes this opportunity to mock all of humanity for having the chutzpah to make any claims to intelligence, suggesting it's probably way beyond our reach. 'Thought is a painful activity,' she writes pityingly. But the thing is, Annabel's learning all the time. There seems to be the glimmer of a chance that stupidity's a temporary state of mind, a void that can be filled. Except maybe in Rome, where Annabel and Frederick are met by a scurrying bunch of ex-pat failures, the talented or once-talented who get by with 'an occasional poem, a job in an art gallery, a part in a film . . . helping a friend move out of a flat without paying the rent . . . a weekend with a Contessa, a week as a guide and escort to a mother and daughter from Rhode Island . . . a tape-recorded interview . . . [or] a montage picture (the tops of mineral-water bottles, mounted on velvet)'. An Eskimo pops up amongst these wannabes, just hanging around: 'a male Eskimo called Gigo whose job ended at that'. It's not easy being a minor character in a Spark novel.

But, *Mamma mia*, motherhood redeems Annabel, not just for the reader but even more so, we're told, in the minds of all the Italians in the book. Spark is clearly amused by the Italian devotion to *bambini* and the *Mamma*, finding motherhood there a guaranteed crowd-pleaser. The newspapers and gossip sheets are full of contrite letters from errant sons to their mothers, and they'll publish 'any story involving mother-love'. Every street corner has its Madonna arch, there's a *pietà* for every picture frame, and a pinch for every baby's cheek. I was in Rome for a year as a child and vividly remember the incessant (well-intentioned) cheek-pinching. I didn't like it so much but, in between, I was taught by a kind waiter how to twirl my spaghetti, which I did appreciate. Children have real standing in Italian society. They are not forgotten appendages. 'It was not customary,' Spark writes of Annabel's Roman community, 'to order children, however naughty, out of one's house, or call them beasts' – whereas in Britain they're always being shoved out of pubs and cafés.

The baby becomes Annabel's ticket back to normality. He makes her feel 'permanently secured to the world'. He's also a very convenient excuse for getting out of things, since in Rome babies come first: 'It was always easy to explain to Italians about a baby's prior claims, which they all conceded without question.' Annabel's serious side, made more potent by motherhood, ensures some resistance to guff. She's no Joan of Arc, this girl, but there's a limit to how much idiocy even she can stand. She rises to the occasion, channelling the Madonna when necessary, and the paparazzi's cameras are 'plucked like guitars and whirled like barrel organs' in celebration.

Annabel's baby and celebrity status both become signs of an emerging personhood. But a public image, says Spark, is always under threat. This makes it rather *like* a baby: something dear to you that you hug to your chest, never trusting anyone else to look after it as well as you can. With luck, nourishment and faithful tending, a baby, *or* a public image, will eventually walk and talk on its own. You just have to set it on its feet. You might then get a good clear spell of camaraderie – before it rebels and never speaks to you again.

Are all movie people idiots? Spark seems to be asking. This novel benefits from another Italian obsession almost equal to the veneration of motherhood: the excitement about cinema, which at times has approached national hysteria. Cinecittá, the movie-industry town in the outskirts of Rome, was built by Mussolini to make propaganda and 'white telephone' movies, but the fact that it was a nationalised film industry allowed other ideas to blossom. The neorealists transformed Italian cinema into high art. Mussolini would have been horrified. And for all her derision of Annabel's film work, it's hard to believe Spark didn't get a kick out of movies like *La Strada*, *La Terra Trema*, *Miracle in Milan*, *Two Women* and the supreme *Bellissima*, where motherhood merges with the slums in a heroic antidote to glitz.

Poor Annabel Christopher – Anna Magnani she ain't. But, given time, better Italian, a painful unrequited passion or two, a little dose of destitution, and more spaghetti, who knows?

I

It was the middle of Friday morning. The sun shone gold-brown on the expanse of parquet floor, in room after room.

The furniture was to be delivered during the course of the following week, some on Monday, some on Thursday, some on Friday.

The English nurse was to arrive on Monday morning.

The housemaid, too, was to come on Monday at eight in the morning. She was to be brought, with all her belongings in her brother's car, which he was ferrying over from Sardinia with the girl, for the occasion.

In Rome it would have been almost ungrateful to expect such plans to move to an orderly conclusion; it was to be expected that some of these arrangements ('Monday for sure . . .' 'Thursday morning – leave it to me.') would start moving anticlockwise at some point.

But for the present, everything had happened that was necessary. Annabel Christopher, the tawny-eyed actress, who in private life was Mrs Frederick Christopher, was aston-ished at the calm achievement so far. For one who was unaccustomed to organise anything, and who was constitu-tionally haphazard, she was astonished at what had in fact come about so far by her own effort, so that it had been pos-sible for her to take on the flat, have it cleaned and painted, decide on the essential minimum furniture necessary for her to move in with her husband and baby, and to make do, picnic-fashion in one room, till the household itself was assembled.

The baby was asleep, tucked into a white pillow. She had laid it on the floor in the big drawing-room. The house was very still. The room where she stood noticing (now that the carpenter's hammer had stopped) the sunlight on the floor, was at the back of the building, removed from the more roisterous traffic of Rome.

The door of the room started to shift open as if moved by a slight breeze. She started walking across the room to close it properly. But in lumbered tall, red-faced Billy O'Brien, her husband's oldest friend. How had he got into the flat? This man irritated her, cropping up as he did. But then, she was relieved to see him for the sake of the news he might have brought.

She said, 'Did I leave the front door open?'

He said, 'Yes,' only, not troubling to explain why he had not, nevertheless, rung the bell. But she had observed before that when people were in process of moving in to a new house, and until the furniture had arrived and been put in place, everyone felt they could come and go, like the workmen and the removal men, without permission. Annabel Christopher's neighbours had already toured the flat, smiling and exclaiming about the beauty of the wallpaper whenever she arrived to see how the work was proceeding.

But she had thought she had closed the front door. Billy stood back against the wall of the room, with the exaggerated deference he had used since she had become the English Lady-Tiger of the films, and, as he always put it, fallen on her feet. Billy was like a worn-out something that one had bought years ago on the hire-purchase system, and was still paying up with no end to it in sight. And again, Billy treated her newly-sprouting film success as a win on the football-pools.

He looked round. He said, 'Is this all in aid of your public image?'

She said, 'Have you seen Frederick?'

Off the screen Annabel Christopher looked a puny little thing, as in fact she had looked on the screen until fairly recently. To those who had not first seen her in the new films, or in publicity pictures, she still looked puny, an English girl from Wakefield, with a peaky face and mousey hair. Billy O'Brien had known her since she was twenty, that is to say, for twelve years. She had then just married his friend Frederick Christopher, with whom he had been to a school of drama. Frederick was then a young actor who had just finished his first season with a repertory theatre. Annabel had played small parts in British films, always being cast as a little chit of a thing, as she was. Presently they were all out of work again and filling in time with temporary jobs. Annabel was a waitress in a coffee-bar. Frederick taught elocution and voice production to a sixth-form group in a grammar school. Billy O'Brien went on the dole, started writing dramatic criticism for little reviews in order to get the theatre tickets, and, since he could not afford to retain his current girl-friend, started up amorous talk with Annabel to see how she would take it. She responded idly with two afternoons in bed with him, after which they got dressed and made the bed. Frederick came home every day talking about voice production. 'Breathing,' he said, 'I emphasise that breathing, breathing, breathing, is the vital factor in voice control. They've got to learn to breathe.' When he found Billy there, he said the same thing, and Annabel made a fresh pot of tea.

Billy went back to Belfast to work in his uncle's grocer's shop for a while, to tide him over the winter. Before he left he told them that he would be slicing bacon all day, as his mother had always wanted him to do. Billy put down his glass of beer and enacted the operation of slicing bacon on a hand-wheel machine, with one hand turning the non-existent handle, and with the other laying the strips of thin, imaginary bacon on a presumed piece of clean grease-proof paper for the customer of his gloomy thoughts. He said, 'My mother wants me to stick in with my uncle, who has no children of his own.' They all laughed. Billy kissed Annabel beerily and departed while they still were all three laughing.

Billy turned up three years later having done many jobs and played many parts in many theatres. He had turned theatre-critic for a new magazine and was now hoping to get a column in a national paper. To this purpose he had prepared a list of people with whom he wanted to obtain interviews.

Annabel was now in demand for small parts in films, always of the same type: she was called for wherever a little slip of a thing was needed – the typist who just happened to return to the office for the parcel she had forgotten when the fatal argument was in progress in the boss's room next door, the little housemaid whose unforeseen amorous exchanges with the delivery boy waylaid the flight plans of the kidnappers, the waif on the underground railway who was one of those who never got home to her lodgings at Poplar; and then she played a more prominent part as the nurse wrongfully accused of stealing drugs, and who woke up by and by in a private room of a hospital in Bangkok, under the watchful eyes of a 'nurse' whom she recognised as a former patient of hers; and she played many other parts. Her eyes were not large, but on the screen they came out so, by some mystery. By some deeper, more involved mystery, another ten years were to pass before Luigi Leopardi, whom many of his friends called 'V' – pronounced 'Voo' – because his real name was Vincenzo, the Italian producer, transformed her eyes, on picture-screens, into those of a Cat-Tiger. (The film company's press secretary first described her as 'The Cat-Tiger' in the publicity that preceded the film *The House on the Piazza* with which she made her first big success. But before her film was released Luigi had changed this to 'English Lady-Tiger', as she was henceforth described on the billing and many other places.)

But in those earlier times when she began to be in demand in English films, she had no means of knowing that she was, in fact, stupid, for, after all, it is the deep core of stupidity that it thrives on the absence of a looking-glass. Her husband, when she was in his company with his men friends, and especially with Billy O'Brien, tolerantly and quite affectionately insinuated the fact of her stupidity, and she accepted this without resentment for as long as it did not convey to her any sense of contempt. The fact that she was earning more and more money than her husband seemed to her at that time a simple proof that he did not want to work. The thought of his laziness nagged her against all contrary evidence and emerged in unpleasant forms, unforeseen moments, embarrassing, sometimes in public, from her sharp little teeth:

'Sorry, I've got to go home to bed. I'm the worker of the family.'

And more and more, Frederick stayed at home all day in their Kensington flat, living on her money, reading book after book – all the books he had never had leisure to read before. He had craved for this contribution to his life. There were few parts suited to his acting talents, so far as talent, continually unapplied, can be said to exist. Frederick, however, held to a theory that a random collision of the natal genes had determined in him a bent for acting only substantial parts in plays by Strindberg, Ibsen, Marlowe and Chekhov (but not Shakespeare); and so far as that went he was right, everything being drably right in the sphere of hypotheses, nothing being measurably or redeemably wrong. In fact, his decision about what parts he was suited to perform on the stage of the theatre did not matter; he was never considered for any parts in the plays he wanted to act in.

By the time he was twenty-nine years of age his undoubted talent had been tested only a few times in small productions and then no more. His mind took the inward turns of a spiral staircase, viewing from every altitude and point of contortion the unblemished, untried, fact of his talent. In reality Frederick was an untrained intellectual. Perhaps he was never happier in his life than in those long mornings at home while reading various literature on the theme of *The Dance of Death*, and annotating Strindberg, while Annabel was at the studios, or was working out of the country for a few weeks, with her meagre skill and many opportunities to exercise it.

He thought of her as doing something far different from anything he wanted to do. She always agreed with him in this, being uncertain, anyway, what he meant. When he talked of 'creating' a role, she agreed with whatever he said about it, because it was something she had heard continually since she attended the school of drama; everyone spoke of creating a role, and of great acting. She had very little apprehension of what they meant. In practice her own instinctive method of acting consisted in playing herself in a series of poses for the camera, just as if she were getting her photograph taken for private purposes. She became skilled at this; she became extremely expert. Ten years later, with the assistance of Luigi Leopardi, she was recognised as a very good actress on the strength of this skill.

In those early days when she was working in small parts her stupidity started to melt; she had not in the least attempted to overcome her stupidity, but she now saw, with the confidence of practice in her film roles, that she had somehow circumvented it. She did not need to be clever, she only had to exist; she did not need to perform, she only had to be there in front of the cameras. She said so to Frederick, as if amazed that she had not thought of it before. He was exasperated, seeing shallowness everywhere:

'You're making a theory, rationalising after the event. You can't act. You're just lucky to get parts.'

'That's what I'm saying.'

It is easy to look back and paint a picture of how things went. At the time it was all unclear.

He became a quarreller, but not with her. And since his anger was not directed against her, but very frequently against others on her behalf, she hardly noticed that he had become a man of angry moods. Only when, on one occasion, he misdirected his protective fury, insulting a film director, did she begin to feel uneasy.

'Why on earth did you say that? He's difficult enough as it is.'

'Well, you complained on and on about him to me. Do you think I want to stand by and see you pushed around?'

She had been grumbling that the director was totally unreasonable, a neurotic, that he drank too much, anyway, and was impossible; she had indulged herself in these grumbles almost as a private and domestic relaxation. Usually, while she was making a film, something happened to upset her; she had got into the habit of bringing back the story to Frederick, as if that was what he was there for. Unawares, she exaggerated; it was for company's sake. But this was the first time he had interfered with her work; it frightened her. 'My career,' she thought, 'my career.' Then she uttered this thought to him. He smiled. She was absolutely bewildered for ten days.

7

He wrote a film script that year, working secretly in her absence. It succeeded, and all to her amazement, made money. That year she had an affair with a solemn American student of drama who had got a small part in one of the films she was playing in. The affair, which lasted two months, and was mostly conducted in such hours of daylight as were available between appearances on the set, ended after she had laughed at him twice because of a look on his face. He was twenty-eight, the same age as herself, and for some years had been obtaining deferment of his obligation to serve in the United States Army in order to complete his dramatic studies in Europe. One day she laughed at him because of his fury and impatience with the telephone exchange; his call-up papers had reached him before he had prepared his application for a further deferment, and that afternoon he was trying to get hold of his lawyer in California; he was shouting to the operator that it was a priority call, it was urgent, it was vital, when she laughed at him the first time. He looked at her in hurt confusion, with the shiny round face of a schoolboy, someone's kid-brother, who (as it might have been) now realised for the first time that his mother hated animals. Annabel did not know why she was laughing, but that was the reason. The second time was when they had been to a film-producer's luncheon, had drunk champagne and then gone to bed at his flat. He got up and went to the bathroom and was sick. He returned to tell her so. She lay back on the pillow, rather sleepy, advised him to lie down, and closed her eyes.

'But I'm sick!' he shouted at her. 'I'm sick!' – so that she opened her eyes and saw him standing on the rug, like a toy doll-man, his arms straight and sticking out from his sides as if they were made of cotton, filled with doll-stuffing and sewn-up. His eyes and mouth seemed completely circular as he stared in the face of her English callousness. She laughed at him the second and last time.

Afterwards he said, 'I'll never forget how you laughed at me when I was sick.'

Presently, when the affair was over, she told Frederick these stories, omitting the parts about bed, regretfully, since the stories seemed to her less amusing without the bed parts. Frederick thought them funny and giggled with her; later however, brooding alone, he wondered how the scene could have been, speculating and wondering and thinking, maybe they were in bed, had been to bed, or were about to get into bed.

But she was glad that her marriage had not broken up as had seemed so likely during these first years of her small successes. Within a few months Frederick was writing another film script; it was one in which she was intended to play the leading part. He now listened more carefully to what she said, and seemed not to think of her as being quite so stupid as before. She thought, after all, he's an interesting man compared with the rest. She liked the fact that his hair, which was slightly crinkly, had begun to turn grey.

Her new professional life had indeed sharpened her wits. She found it exciting. She found it frightening. She clung to Frederick, and even to his old friends who came and went to and from their lives, and especially did she adhere to Billy O'Brien, who, she felt, kept Frederick happy when she was away from home.

Billy taunted, resented, and even simply insulted her. She put up with it because of old times; he was one of the last remnants of a past life she had not known at the time had been as good as it already seemed in retrospect. Now she had more money, more letters, more business, more to talk and think about. In those days, she had written a letter

9

sometimes on odd afternoons, to her father, or to a cousin or a school friend. She had written it by hand, sealed it, carried it to the post office, had bought one postage stamp which she licked, placed on the envelope, and thumped firm; she had then borne the letter to the letterbox and dropped it in with a plop. This most satisfying series of actions was now lost to her for ever. She now thought with kindness rather than regret, of those long letters about nothing much, and the posting of them, and the return from the letter-box to put the kettle on for tea.

Once, when he came home late with Billy – towards two o'clock in the morning – she said sentimentally, 'It was lovely in the old days when I used to write one letter sometimes and go out and put it in the box; just one letter. And then –'

'Oh, stop posing,' Billy said. She was standing on the carpet, one hand on a side-table, gazing back into her youth, as if playing a middle-aged part.

'I'm not posing,' she said, and flopped into a chair, 'I used to love to post a letter, that's all.'

Frederick was slightly drunk and was now drinking a whisky and soda. He said, 'She thinks I'm her letter-box, a solid bright red pillar-box to post her letters in. That's what she wants a husband for.'

She went to bed quickly, not wanting to indulge her desire to prolong the argument and perhaps get involved in a row. She would have liked a row, but she had to be up at seven the next morning to be on the set, bright-eyed, by eight. Frederick was seldom drunk. Usually he tolerated Billy's baiting attitude towards her but did not join in.

But time became a hunted animal; there was no time to write so many letters. A secretary from the film studios came to her rescue when the papers piled up beyond bearing, and answered them largely in her own way. An agency methodically settled her working days and the payments for her hours of hire. These payments were large, still larger per week than those that Frederick, feverish at his film scripts, could earn in several months.

The time was still to come when she could look back even at these years with the same nostalgia as she now felt towards the time of the one postage stamp. She was to look back with amazed and incomprehensible pangs to their time of casual secretarial arrangements, to the haphazard series of housemaids and household-helps, her happiness at getting so much film work to do, her comparatively trivial successes and to the way she had circumvented her stupidity so far that she could entertain Frederick with that story of the Californian student and how funny he had looked.

The script Frederick wrote for her towards her thirtieth year was set in Rome where they had lingered sometimes on their summer holidays, breathing the uninhibited air of the Italian film world, and magnetised by the café life of the Via Veneto where everyone who was not a tourist was in, or wanted to be in, a film. They also toured the ruins and the places of antiquity. In the film that Frederick devised for Annabel she was to appear as an English governess who had been taken to live in Rome by her American employers, the family of a diplomat with three children.

Thought is a painful activity. Frederick had largely given it up, and, guiltily concealing this fact from himself, had opened his feelings to pain. He was easily hurt. When Annabel, on reading the script, said, 'It's good, it's like *The Turn of the Screw*, isn't it?' he was furious.

'What the hell do you mean? You haven't read *The Turn of the Screw*.'

'No, but I saw the movie. I only meant the film. But I like your script. I like it. It's like *The Turn of the Screw* in significance only, that's all, and that's what I like about it.'

He took the script from her hand with ominous care and consideration; then said in the tones of a phoneticist addressing an illiterate foreigner, 'Will you do me a favour, Annabel?'

'I don't know,' she said, glaring dangerously into his face with an expression that looked sickly-eyed, although it was the same expression that later was to come out, by the best colour methods of the cinema, so fiery and so marvellous.

He continued to enunciate. 'Please do not talk of "significance", because you do not understand it. And that is because you are insignificant yourself.'

Annabel said immediately, 'D'you think so? Oh, well, minority opinions are always interesting.' This was her latest manner of response; she had recently been exposed to the influence of a new set of young friends, celebrities mainly by virtue of being the children of celebrated or famously rich people, and among them particularly was Golly Mackintosh, an heiress of twenty-two from the Philippine Islands, who had a head of young, grey-tinted hair, and who responded to the world as charmingly and heartlessly as a flower. Golly had a way of flipping back a pellet-like word or two when challenged by any criticism whatsoever, or by any praise whatsoever, and Annabel had picked up the habit from her with rapid intuition, as if Golly was a school of drama.

Perceiving all this, Frederick was continually overcome by a dazzled exasperation at her capacity for achieving the most impressive effects by the most superficial means. He was infuriated that anyone should be deceived by her. He was firm in his opinion that an actor should be sincere in the part he played, and should emotionally experience whatever he was to portray, from the soul outward. Even in her acting, he thought, Annabel is a sort of cheat, she acts from a sense of manners only.

'You never feel the part, do you?' he had said.

'I don't know what you mean,' she said. 'When I'm acting I'm working. What do you mean? One has got to play the part at the time.'

He wanted to leave her, and made up his mind that he would do so, eventually. Eventually, he thought, I'll have to go. But, in a way, he was hypnotised by a sense of the enormity of her deception, the more her reputation grew and she accepted it as part of her rightful earnings. Whenever any of his old friends began to suggest that her acting had some depth, or charm, or special merit, he silently nurtured the atrocity, reminding himself that nobody but he could know how shallow she really was. I know her, he thought, inside out. They don't.

She was as unaware of his secret life as she was of her own, for hers was not articulate. She probably never formed a sentence in her mind that she would hesitate to reveal to the open air. But her secret purposes, too, took shape none the less. And, in the economy of things, these secrecies of the heart were not in themselves a bad basis for married love. They always patched up their rows, went out together, were accustomed to each other. Moreover, they were proud of each other in the eyes of their expanding world where he was considered to be deeply interesting and she highly talented.

Frederick's script was accepted for production with Annabel as the star. It was her most important part, so far. The film companies who backed it told him they could take a chance on Annabel, because a film made in Italy could be a low-budget film.

2

It was a scene in the governess film Frederick had written for her, *The House on the Piazza*, that spread fire in the imagination of Luigi Leopardi. He had a small financial interest in this film and was watching the shooting at the Bernini fountain in the Piazza Navona. At this point in the film story, Frederick's script had been to various alteration-hands; and the final version approved by the American Corporation which was putting the bulk of the money into it at first moved Frederick to request that his name be removed from the billing. But later, when publicity for the film became rife, he got his name put back again.

At that moment when Luigi Leopardi noticed her, Annabel's role as an English governess had progressed to a point where she was shown to slip out of the house one hot, still night, and gone to dance in the plashing bowl of the great Bernini fountain in the Piazza Navona, to cool off the passion she had conceived for the master of the house (whose wife was carrying on with an Italian painter, anyway – at the insistence of the film company's directors, who felt that her infidelity made her husband's affair with Annabel more moral). This harmless film made Annabel's reputation, although it was itself rather lifeless. The public did not throng. The company lost money. Frederick blamed the changed script, the direction, the photography, the male cast, the too over-characterised child players, and he blamed Annabel for playing up to the public image that was forming around her, starting in the Italian picture magazines and moving westward and westward. He said that she had exploited her public image at the expense of the film as a whole.

He waited three weeks from the release of the film to say these things, and his manner was calm and almost disinterested, as if he were discussing some other film they had seen together. She listened with a vague ear, for she was curled up on the sofa among the blue chintz roses, in the house in Surrey that they had now acquired, reading through a batch of the latest reviews of the film from the monthly magazines, provincial papers, and journals of smaller circulation. They had just arrived in the post. She did not read each one from beginning to end, but rummaged rapidly with her eyes, ignoring for the moment all the brightly metaphorical criticism of construction and plot, and seizing on everything that concerned herself and her performance. 'She is a twentieth-century Jane Eyre' . . . 'She is certainly a "tiger in the tank"' . . . 'Though this movie was a poor vehicle for her talents Annabel did a remarkable job of pulling it together. The scene in the garden where she glides into the children's secret lair with an expression of terrifying serenity . . . the effect of external propriety with a tiger in her soul . . . something between Jane Eyre, a heroine of D.H. Lawrence, and the governess in *The Turn of the Screw*. The children, alas . . .' One review was headed 'Should a Husband Write a Film Script for His Own Wife?' The last of the batch was from a Belfast weekly paper on which Billy O'Brien had a film-critic's column. Billy wrote:

Annabel Christopher's performance is a *chef-d'oeuvre* which is also a *succès d'estime*. Although she will never make the big-star grade she has an undeniable presence, a *je ne sais quoi*. But this film was, in fact, beyond Miss Christopher's grasp. It *could* have been a great movie, had the casting . . . Needless to say, the intelligence of the dialogue was wasted . . .

Annabel heard Frederick's voice continuing, as she read these reviews, its dispassionate analysis and sensed a bitterness that she had been expecting. She said, 'What's wrong with a public image?' and put Billy's review on one side, because it sounded rather funny and she intended to read it, over the telephone, to Golly Mackintosh as soon as possible. 'What's wrong with a public image?' she said to Frederick.

She looked at him and was taken more than ever by his role as a man of theory – for she thought of appearances in this way, they were 'roles'; and whether or not he was a man of theory was irrelevant. His actor's good looks had sunk into his cheek-bones and eye-sockets. As her husband, he presented a very good public image indeed.

Very young girls, young actresses and starlets, were especially attracted to him because of his seriousness. He had slept with a few of them, and one in particular, a long-haired peach-like beauty whom he was at this moment very tempted to go and live with.

Every few weeks he wanted to leave Annabel. At the same time that he encouraged her affection, he feared it, because it was of a type to undermine his seriousness. She had said lately to him, as earlier he had said to her, 'Oh, come off that pose.' To which he had replied, 'Pose? Do you think everything's done for effect simply because you have no other motive?' She had said, 'Why can't you be human like you used to be?' And he had replied, 'You mean *as* I used to be.'

Annabel at least understood that if only for effect, he had cultivated a private self-image of seriousness, and that she was a threat to it. But she was now very prosperous; his attractive intellectual aspect and the dignity it gave to his life depended greatly on her earnings.

He was dazzled by her unconcern about this; he was puzzled. It was unlike the former times, when she would say, 'I've got to go home to bed. I'm the worker of the family.' Now it was only unthinkingly that she referred to her money. He was awed by her business sense, if that was what dictated her disregard of his living on her earnings. She could afford him at the price; he was no longer a problem. Was that how Annabel saw their position? He was puzzled, impressed, and recurrently resentful. At any moment she could change her mind. She could turn. But she went on regardless, and he meditated upon her equilibrium. And again, he was jealous of other men around her.

But they probably would have separated now, had it not been for Annabel's triumph in her next film, *Minerva Arrived at Platform 10*, when she became fixed in the public imagination as the English Tiger-Lady, so that both of their personal lives became from a few weeks' exposure on the covers and within the pages of the world's popular magazines, a trailing extension of the film.

They lived in rooms in a hotel in Rome during the shooting of *Minerva Arrived at Platform 10*. Frederick had not written this script, but for some reason connected with the evasion of Annabel's income tax, he had been put on the pay-roll as an 'adviser' to the film. He did not attempt to advise, but had found friends of his own in Rome.

Billy O'Brien followed them and was looking around for jobs in films. He sometimes gave lessons in voice-production to English drama students and lessons in English to Italian actors. Frederick was particularly enchanted by Luigi's press secretary, a very small Italian woman of twenty-eight, who had broken away from her family to take up a career. She knew she was good at her job and had pined for more scope, which she now found in her commission to build up Annabel. Her name was Francesca.

Frederick was fascinated by Francesca's newly-emancipated zeal, special to Italian girls who had taken an unheard-of flat of their own, lived with lovers, and worked with intensity for long hours and poor wages. In Francesca, this combined with a convent-trained reticence and an old-rooted deference to men; she even gave a kind of instinctive precedence to a male cat over a female cat. She was clever at her job.

It was Francesca who, having decided without hesitation that her job with Luigi was more valuable to her than Frederick as a lover would be, decided on the securest course of action for herself, combining it, in the economy of her quick little brain, with the most brilliant line of publicity in the interests of Luigi's film; she made Frederick and Annabel into a famous couple, impeccably formal by the light of day, voluptuously enamoured with each other under cover of night. She knew the Italian magazines as well as they knew themselves, which is to say they knew no other type of vitality than theirs, and this was their strength, for these sunny glossies of Italy beamingly scandalised the just and the unjust alike, churning up the splendour of their wickedness, weekly. The range of emotions was as grand as Grand Opera, but no subtler. A clandestine child, preferably a son, of a film star is discovered; or an opera singer tells of the persecution she currently endures at the hands of the tenor's wife (under the headline 'Assunta is Jealous of Me'); divorce in a royal family is a standard thriller, or any story involving mother-love, especially when the theme turns on the sacrifice of a steady lover. Sheer villains, utter innocents – the world's most complicated celebrities have been cast anew in these simple roles.

In fact, it is only a country of dramatic history, cradled in the Seven Capital Sins, that could so full-heartedly produce this popular art-form; the Seven Capital Sins being pride, covetousness, lust, anger, gluttony, envy and sloth. Never a week but one of these pure vices formed the topic of a new sensation at the time Annabel Christopher's public image was launched and beyond that time. For these happy launchings were inevitably presented with the optimism of Act I, but bearing within them all the potentials of Act III and its doomed revelations, sooner or later. The contrary cardinal virtues were, as almost everywhere, ignored except in the flagrant flouting, the only virtue which was exploited being forgiveness, and this was passionately spread over the pages, most popular being forgiving wives and mothers.

To start in this setting was a good start. If the stories caught on at all they caught on well. Germany and France picked them up. In slow whispers, and in more sophisticated accents, they seeped westward. It is a mistake to think that sensational publications start in America. They end there, in a somewhat tired form. But they start, classic, innocent, thoughtless and young, in Italy, the Motherland of Sensation.

Annabel got her good start. Luigi's press secretary, Francesca, presented her, as everyone in the world of journalism agreed, with a new and brilliant slant that launched, they said, both actress and film. And Francesca, euphoric in her success, was even more daemonically urged by her sacrifice of Frederick as a potential lover; anything rather than go back to her family. She now vicariously made Annabel inextricable from Frederick. Francesca brought him into the story. She ranged among Luigi's press photographers until she found the one with the least ideas of his own. Then she posed the couple for him according to her own ideas. She brought Frederick into the picture as well as the story. She arranged the press interviews and supervised the press photographers. She was always there. She wrote some of the stories herself – in what hours of the night? She briefed the journalists and arranged the public image of Annabel Christopher and husband to Luigi's extreme satisfaction, which he did not too warmly express lest Francesca should start thinking something of her abilities.

Frederick hardly knew what was going on. He was still fascinated by Francesca, and then he was fascinated by her plump sister who had an indeterminate clerical job in a back office of the film studios, and then he was attracted to her fair, lean brother for whom Francesca was trying hard to get a part in a film, and who hung round the sets all the time. There was generally a family air about the place. Francesca was only one of those Italian girls there who had officially left their families, and it would not have occurred to any of them who boasted of having broken from family life not to include their cousins, brothers and sisters in their new lives, or try to get them jobs.

Frederick did not quite realise at the time how deeply involved with Annabel's public image he was becoming at Francesca's hands. He took it for granted that he should be photographed with Annabel and that they should be interviewed together. After all, he was an actor, too. He laughed at the magazine stories and thought them childish and therefore harmless, a mistake in logic.

He wandered among the empty sets in the large film-studio location in the suburbs of Rome. This environment was comparatively new to him, he had never acted in films.

Once, passing a plate-glass door he saw a large, fair, dreamy-eyed poet whom he had met recently at a party. The poet was reading something written on a sheet of paper. He was surrounded by other men who looked like assistant producers. A girl sat meekly at a desk. The poet's lips moved silently as he read; then he said something that Frederick could not hear through the door. The men started talking, too, but the poet, still dreamy-eyed, had lifted a thin alabaster ashtray and smashed it on the floor.

There was a flurry of calming hands. Frederick moved on.

Another day, he had to pass through a room in which were two men, one lolling carelessly on a sofa and the other standing jumpily beside him, screaming at him. Frederick understood enough Italian at that time to overhear: 'You're not serious. We're serious here. You drink little cups of tea all day. Little cups of tea . . .' They neither of them took the slightest notice of Frederick as he passed. The man on the sofa reached out his foot in a bored way and placed it on a convenient chair while the hysteric went on, 'Little cups of tea . . .' As he reached the far door Frederick heard the other reply, 'I'm not English, I'm a Filipino.'

A glimpse here and there, and then, with Francesca, the noise of excited Italian voices everywhere immediately delighted Frederick. Following which, within a few hours, he turned bitter, like one suffering abruptly from drink. He turned sourly to Annabel, telling her what an idiot's world this Italian film-world was. He said he, too, would become a moron if he stayed on much longer. Usually she replied that she was sick of him.

But then Francesca would come, either to talk to them, or to arrange an interview, or with a photographer to take a picture of Annabel lounging on the bed, in her nightdress, one shoulder-band slipping down her arm and her hair falling over part of her face. Francesca disarranged the bed. She sat Frederick on the edge of the bed, in a Liberty dressing-gown, smoking, with a smile as of recent reminiscence. Or else Francesca had them photographed with a low table set with a lace-edged tray of afternoon tea, and the sun streaming in the window. Frederick held his cup and seemed to be stirring it gently and gravely while Annabel, sweet but unsmiling, touched the silver teapot with a gracious hand. 'We must get the two sides of your lives,' Francesca explained, in case there should be any doubt.

Annabel was entirely aware of the image-making process in every phase. She did not expect this personal image to last long in the public mind, for she intended to play other parts than that of the suppressed tiger, now that she was becoming an established star.

Twice Frederick went off for two days with Billy O'Brien. When he did this, Francesca was more worried than Annabel, who was working and hardly noticed his absence.

He was beginning to see that Francesca would never sleep with him, neither she nor any of her relatives, for, as if by her command, they always evaded the question and started to speak of Annabel.

Well, in the event, Frederick found himself rooted deeply and with serious interest in a living part such as many multitudes believe exists: a cultured man without a temperament, studious, sportsman-like, aristocratic, and a fatherly son of Mother Earth, Annabel's husband. As for Annabel, she was portrayed cool and equal to him in all these respects, except that she was a tiger-woman at heart and in 'the secret part of their lives'. This tiger was portrayed only by her eyes; it was an essential of the public image that the tiger quality was always restrained in public. Within a few weeks, throughout Italy and beyond, it was decidedly understood, thoroughly suggested, hinted and memorised, that in private, inaccessible to all possible survey, and particularly in bed, Annabel Christopher, the new star who played the passionate English governess, let rip. She was presented, now, as every man's perfect wife, with her composed and conventional appearance. Frederick Christopher's wife was both envied and worshipped. And the more sophisticated readers simply repeated the Italian proverb 'If it isn't true, it's to the point.'

It was somehow felt that the typical Englishman, such as Frederick Christopher was, had always really concealed a foundry of smouldering sex beneath all that expressionless reserve. It was suggested in all the articles that cited the Christopher image, that this was a fact long known to the English themselves, but only now articulated. Later, even some English came to believe it, and certain English wives began to romp in bed far beyond the call of their husbands, or the capacities of their years, or any of the realities of the situation.

Minerva Arrives at Platform 10 was made, released, and applauded. Sexy Annabel was now photographed for nice English magazines and was shown on television, at the races, wearing a country coat and a meek brimmed hat, looking intently at horses only, while Frederick, with his back turned to her, was talking without animation to another, equally phlegmatic male of the same excitingly hypocritical breed. Francesca's presentation had caught on. Once, when interviewed, Frederick said, 'Well, we've been married twelve years, and we get along together; that's all there is to it.' This was taken to be an example of British understatement by everyone who had seen and who had not yet seen Annabel's third film, *The Tiger-Lady*.

The gossip columns said that Frederick was to play a leading part opposite Annabel in her next film.

He decided to leave Annabel.

They went to Hollywood. He was to be tried out for the part. On the way, on the aeroplane, when they were talking in quite a friendly manner, again he privately decided to part from her.

After being tested in every possible way he did not get the part. He wasn't a film actor, really, Annabel said. The producer, anxious to keep peace for quite normal reasons besides those connected with Annabel's public image, told Frederick he was too good an actor for this sort of thing.

In fact he could have played the part well had he not been inhibited by the idea of revolt from his marriage.

He was now so settled in a daily determination to end the marriage, call off the public image, declare it null and void, that he did not see the point of doing anything about it just yet, especially as it would be construed as a gesture of disappointment at not getting the part. He settled into a routine of deciding to break with Annabel, and to wait until they had left these gossipy circles.

He waited for Annabel, again hanging round the studios, and always on the set when she was being filmed. She realised that he was obsessed with her.

Another leading man played the part of the Tiger-Lady's lover. Annabel was now part of a world of Oscars and film festival prizes; although she was not yet cited for any of these awards, still she was assumed to be in the running for them.

She was seen in public only with Frederick, and then she wore discreet, well-cut linear evening dresses with a rope of pearls. The pearls, too, became famous, although they were quite an ordinary string of pearls.

But Frederick's misery began to show in his face. He spent a lot of time with the director's wife, an elegant woman from South Carolina who looked, and was, far more of a Tiger and a Lady than was Annabel. The film company was concerned lest a break in the famous marriage should take place before the release of the new picture, and spoke plainly to Annabel on this point. It was all a matter of timing, said their spokesman, in the confident, fatherly manner of the expert in timing of stars' divorces.

Whereupon Annabel took fright at the whole mythology that had vapoured so thickly about her, and turned to Frederick in real panic. They started sleeping together again, having by mutual agreement, and on the grounds of nervous exhaustion, slept apart for the past few months.

'I said,' said Annabel, 'that we were free to get divorced if we want to.'

'Quite bloody right,' he said. 'If we don't draw the line now, they've got us trapped.'

Soon it was rumoured that Annabel had decided to save her marriage by having a baby. It was represented everywhere as her decision, which infuriated Frederick. Twice he made huge scenes in public. Then he was infuriated by Annabel's alarm. A proper wife would have pacified him, not remonstrated with him about what people would say. He said, 'All you think of is your public image.'

'No. I'm thinking of the baby,' she said. 'I shouldn't have trouble at a time like this.'

'And the baby,' he said, 'the baby's only in aid of your public image.'

'What's wrong with my public image?' she said. 'It's a good one. I'm a faithful wife, not a tart.'

The fatherly executive at the studios said to Annabel, 'Your husband should have help.'

'What with?' she said.

'He should see a psychiatrist.'

'Tell him that yourself, to his face. Don't tell me. Tell him, and see what happens.'

She did not repeat this conversation to Frederick for fear of another scene. In the meantime he was pacified by the fact that he was still an idol of the young people who were everywhere in this environment. The children of film people and their friends, occupying unimportant jobs or merely decorating the passing scene.

The fright that had brought Annabel and Frederick together did not last. Annabel finished the film before the baby began to show. They returned to England, soberly, as after a hangover, on the old *Queen Mary*.

By the time the baby was born, the high boom of the Christopher cult had passed, which meant that the image was established. They agreed to stay together for the baby's sake. Frederick privately decided to leave Annabel in a few months' time, when she was to go to Italy to appear in another picture. Meantime he wrote a film script for an English company; it might have been a suitable film for Annabel, but the company put another actress in the part; Frederick suspected, but could not prove, that she had turned it down.

Billy O'Brien came back and forth into their lives; he rarely came without asking for a loan. Annabel, who was becoming very rich, objected to these loans. It was the only expenditure of Frederick's that she could not bear. He said it was his own money he was lending, and if she wanted to abandon old friends like Billy O'Brien, then she could count him out as well.

She found a job for Billy in Rome, teaching voice-production to English student-priests in a seminary, for she wanted to go there with her baby boy, and she wanted Frederick to be with her. She did not want to change her public image just yet.

Frederick looked at her as she suckled the baby and said, 'He fits in with your public image.' But it was not that the baby fitted the public image, it was rather that the image served the child so well. She was enamoured with this baby and was determined not to be left by Frederick in the first years of the child's life to look round for a new husband, a new type of film, form a new household, change her successful public image for another or, possibly, no image at all. Not yet, she thought; not yet.

She arranged for Frederick to get commissions to write film scripts in Italy. She persuaded him to move there, settle there with her, at least for three years while she did some films with Luigi.

Frederick said, 'You're in love with "V".'

She said, 'Why do you call him "V"? It's only awful people, those awful people round him wanting bits of jobs for their kids who call him "V" – and wanting to get a cut out of the price of film-sets – people like that nasty little Alessandro who cheated him over the plastic for Hampton Court when I played the reunion scene in *Minerva* – I am not in love with Luigi.'

'Then what does it matter what I call him?'

'Needless to say, I don't let anyone call you "Fred" or "Freddie" in my hearing; I always stop them.'

'If it's needless to say, why do you say it?'

The Christophers' move to Italy found great approval there; Luigi Leopardi was waiting for Annabel to play in his new film; many other directors wanted Frederick's scripts, for his plays were well-informed and could be had cheaply. In fact Frederick's scripts were a kind of readers' digest. He was happy with an Italian girl called Marina, whose family lived in the country. Marina had good looks and sharp intelligence.

She had a flat of two rooms in a modern tenement in the suburbs of Rome. He saw Marina frequently and always secretly. She understood the importance of marriage to everyone, let alone Frederick Christopher, and was content with his love-visits.

Annabel and Frederick were photographed by the arrangement of Francesca on their walks around Rome; they leant on monuments, dallied at fountains, or were seen in perspective through the dramatic archway of the Via Giulia, in the colourful market of the Campo dei Fiori, or ambling with the Saturday crowds down the Via Coronari. They were seen dining in the spring air in the squares of Trastevere, or in the Piazza Navona. They visited churches, the tombs of the apostles and martyrs, and they were photographed together as the marvellous couple with the secret of happy marriage, on the Spanish steps.

On her own initiative, and to Francesca's proud satisfaction, Annabel found a flat and started to furnish it. Meantime, they occupied a set of rooms in a hotel.

She was photographed at the shops, buying curtain materials and a washing-machine. Everyone said that these English tigresses knew how to hold their husbands, that was the reason Englishmen did not frequent prostitutes or keep mistresses. Much photographed, Frederick in correct morning suit and Annabel shrouded in black lace set out to be received by the Pope, and half an hour later were equally photographed on their emergence from the Vatican doors.

Luigi was told by Annabel that his press secretary's services would be highly unwelcome if she attempted to bring the baby into this parade. Accordingly, no photographers approached the baby, except by chance in the gardens of the Villa Borghese. Annabel gave out a few charming photographs of the baby, Carl, to the press, through Francesca. Annabel had taken them herself.

She was not in love with Luigi Leopardi, but she found him dependable. He was not at all concerned or cynical about the difference between her private life and her public image; he did not recognise that any discrepancy existed. He said, 'What is personality but the effect one has on others? Life is all the achievement of an effect. Only the animals remain natural.' He told her that personality was different from a person's character, but even character could change over the years, depending on the habits one practised. 'I see no hypocrisy in living up to what the public thinks of you,' he said. 'What do they think? – That you have been married for twelve years? Well, it's true, isn't it?'

'But I'm not a Tiger-Lady,' she said.

'Aren't you? Come and live a little with me and you soon will be.'

'I doubt it.'

'Before I made you the Tiger-Lady, you didn't even look like a lady in public, never mind a tiger in private. It's what I began to make of you that you've partly become.'

Before she realised her mistake she had opened her cloudy eyes, which were so luminous on the screen, and said quite cheerfully, 'Well, isn't that the theme of *Pygmalion*?' She spoke a fraction too soon, because, by the time she recalled how furious Frederick had been that time she had said of his script 'It's a bit like *The Turn of the Screw*, isn't it?' Luigi was already talking defensively ('ten to the dozen', as she said later, describing her lapse to Frederick in an effort to humour him by putting herself some little bit in the wrong). Luigi, ten to the dozen, refuted the imputation that any idea of his was not absolutely original. This cloudburst passed. Annabel finally promised to do Luigi's new picture, as indeed, she had intended to do, but had withheld confirmation for some months. And she said she was too tired to go to bed with him. She telephoned to the hotel, where a temporary nurse was left in charge of the baby, to see how he was. She did this every three hours from wherever she happened to be.

The baby, Carl, was the only reality of her life. His existence gave her a sense of being permanently secured to the world which she had not experienced since her own childhood had passed. She was so enamoured of the baby that she did not want to fuss over it with gurgles and baby-babble, as did the nurse and the secretaries who came from the studio. She felt a curious fear of display where the baby was concerned, as if this deep and complete satisfaction might be disfigured or melted away by some public image.

Luigi offered her a share of his bed for sleeping purposes only, since she was so tired. But she left his flat early, explaining that she had to be with the baby. It was always easy to explain to Italians about a baby's prior claims, which they all conceded without question, no matter how many nurses and baby-sitters one could afford. She thought this was probably why she had brought the child here; it was a move similar to that of hiding an infant in the bulrushes.

Annabel was still a little slip of a thing, but her face had changed, as if by action of many famous cameras, into a mould of her public figuration. She looked aloof and well bred. Her smile had formerly been quick and small, but now it was slow and somewhat formal; nowadays she was vivacious only when the time came, in front of the cameras, to play the tiger.

Luigi had found out for her one thing she had wanted to know. Who was Frederick's mistress in Rome? A girl in the suburbs, quite poor, a young typist called Marina, very pretty. Frederick took reasonable care not to be noticed by the neighbours, usually he wore dark glasses, always arriving late when most of those people were in bed. Annabel was relieved, for she had feared he was having an affair with someone spectacular, a princess or an opera singer, who might easily turn their public image into a shambles, an ugly mess. Annabel knew very well that this image would come to an end sooner or later, just as she assumed that, sooner or later, she would have a real affair with Luigi. But it was necessary to do one more Tiger-Lady film before taking action in her marriage; then, perhaps some subtle change could be made, either in her life or in the mind of her public. At this point it was both inconceivable to her that Frederick should not continue to be her husband, and inconceivable that they could live on together, like this, without love, but only a dependency on each other. Smiling slowly when she was recognised by some passers-by as she got into her car, she felt serene and confident. She had never been given to problems.

She had never been given to problems, which was why she had a reputation among her acquaintances for facing and solving them.

She had an older sister, married to a businessman in Canada. Her mother was dead. Her father had married again. Her old friends were now very few; her success had suddenly put a distance between her and them, it had created that awkwardness in meeting again, as if after returning from a very long absence. But even her old friends now, those whom she was unlikely to meet in the film studios, swore that Annabel had always had a tremendous business capacity, had coped with complex problems, faced them, solved them. Even to them, she had become a sort of strong-woman, a sort of tiger at heart. She was not sure that they were not right, because she was not sure what a problem was. Maybe I am strong, she had thought, when she arranged, all on her own, to buy the flat. She spoke Italian ungrammatically but fluently, accompanied by appropriate gestures, exactly as if she were acting a part as an Italian. Something about this act of miming, and the rattle of her tongue as the words came out, influenced her to think somewhat in the Italian mode. At all events, she managed to engage a lawyer and acquire the flat, both at a good price. This was a more difficult feat for a foreigner, and a famous one, and moreover, a woman, than she knew.

Until recently her world of people had been full of mutual assistance on all practical matters, and Frederick and his friends had in any case done the talking. Mostly, now, she had paid professional help for everything necessary to life. It was fate, part of the distance from life that had occurred at the same time as the close-ups on the screen. And she started making her arrangements from that point.

One day she said to an interviewer from a woman's journal who had asked her what success meant:

'It means that your friends don't bring you back silk scarves from their holidays any more.'

'Really? Why not?' said the interviewer, her pencil poised like an excited nose over the floppy notebook which was perched on the arm of the chair.

Realising that she had somehow made a statement with a weight of significance, Annabel quickly said, 'Well, I suppose they haven't got my address, I've been moving about so much lately, Hollywood, and so on.'

'Oh, I see. So when you've settled down, you'll be getting silk scarves again? You like silk scarves, brightly coloured ones? . . . Would you say you have a collection? . . . Do you give scarves as presents? . . . Are your favourite silk scarves those over there? Does your husband wear silk scarves? . . .'

Billy O'Brien had acquired in Rome that circle of international people whose kind are round and about in every junction of the world, and who are interconnected with interchangeable artistic professions. These were the young and ageing actor-painters, painter-architects, architect-writers, writer-guitarists and other, more ramified, combines of Rome. There were very few whose talents, in themselves, were poor, given faith, hope and single-mindedness – and, given the necessary opportunity, or, as it might be, the gift for seeking and grasping opportunities, any one of these versatile people might have done well in any one field. However, all that had not been to be, and so here they were in Rome puttering away their inheritance of grace with an occasional poem, a job in an art gallery, a part in a film which no more than entailed sitting at a café table for six hours, a morning's effort at helping a friend to move out of a flat without paying the rent, a paid-for trip to Paris, a weekend with a Contessa, a week as a guide and escort to a mother and daughter from Rhode Island in the United States of America, a tape-recorded interview, a montage picture (the tops of mineral-water bottles, mounted on velvet), and the restoration of antique furniture. Among Billy's acquaintance were also critics of all things and nationalities, translators, young Americans in Rome for their education, four Italian ladies of middle age, who had achieved emancipation and beyond, and who were regarded by their families and Italian friends with abhorrent respect, and there was also a male Eskimo called Gigo whose job ended at that.

Annabel had frigidly met, or at least been briefly in the company of, this set, one evening after dinner shortly upon their arrival in Rome, when Frederick had taken her to Billy O'Brien's flat. They were very tightly squeezed into it, for it was a small flat in a narrow street in the old quarter. The neighbours shouted from the windows for quietness; one by one the windows had gone up and the heads had appeared. Someone said to Annabel, 'Hey, Tiger!' She had said she had to get home to the baby, and had run away, all down the black, narrow stairs and the dark streets, till she came to a main street and eventually got a taxi. Frederick had not come home for two nights.

She was visited the next day, however, by Billy O'Brien, who had demanded a reason for her sudden departure. Her film-employers and agents, and many of her new successful friends in the acting profession, had warned her not to be involved with mobs of people who would gossip and destroy her image. She felt that Frederick had been testing her, to see what she would do. She had said to Billy, on that occasion, 'I had to get back to the baby.' This was as true a reason as any of them. He had said, 'Why did you come, then?' She said, 'Oh, we only looked in. I didn't know there was a party.' She loathed Billy, but could not fall out with him. He knew more about Frederick, now, than she did.

3

Again, Frederick was away somewhere; he had not shown up for five days and nights. Tonight would be the sixth. She had moved from the hotel, but had left messages there. He knew, anyway, that she was camping in the flat, alone with the baby, for the weekend. It was the middle of Friday morning. The spring sunshine touched the parquet floors. The bulk of the furniture was still to be delivered. The English nurse and the housemaid from Sardinia were expected on Monday.

The neighbours had come and gone with offers of help, promises of future domestic services, and threats of future company all day and every day. Annabel's flat was on the first floor of a sixteenth-century *palazzo* of mixed tenantry, the very rich, the comparatively so, the very poor, and the comparatively so. The older inhabitants were rather poor, living there with their families and in-laws intact, in some of the flats at the old fixed rent, the more recent being bespectacled lawyers, or Americans who had restored the great sixteenth-century rooms to graciousness, with central heating and air-conditioning. The views from Annabel's flat were many and magnificent. Annabel was not yet informed precisely on the nature and dates of everything outside her windows, but she said often, 'I can feel the atmosphere.' She knew by heart the dome of St Peter's and Castel Sant' Angelo. She had a guide-book, which seemed to her to lack the atmosphere of the actual decor, and even that did not cover every tower, fountain, church, column and palace visible across the piazza, or, on the other sides, where her windows opened out into little balconies, to be seen through the slits between houses, those narrow lanes intertwining with narrow lanes, the twisty minds of history.

The flat was empty, waiting for furniture. The baby was tucked into a makeshift bed on the floor.

Billy O'Brien had let himself in like a draught of wind. Frederick had evidently given him the door-key. His arrival at the flat that afternoon upset her, but now again she was anxious for news of Frederick. She looked at the baby on the floor. He was sleeping. She said, 'Don't wake Carl. Come into the kitchen.' Mostly, the kitchen furniture had already been moved in.

Billy tramped after her, heavily, as if he had every right to wake the baby, and more right to be there than she had. He said, 'I'd like bacon and eggs. Have you got bacon and eggs?' She was about to suggest telephoning to a restaurant to order a meal to be sent, but was anxious to placate Billy, hoping for news of Frederick. Her script was lying on one of the kitchen tables, her new script. Billy lifted it and started to read it, standing by the refrigerator, while she fried his eggs and bacon. She was furious. She said, 'I was learning my part, my lines.'

He laughed out loud without giving a reason for it, then went on peering at the script with his sandy eyes, turning over the pages with his large freckled hand.

She said, 'Where's Frederick?'

He said, '*The Staircase* – is that the name of your next film?'

She said, 'No. That's only provisional.'

He sat down at the table where she had laid a place with the stainless steel knives and forks she had brought to the house for a start, and placed the script on the table beside him. She said, 'That script is supposed to be top secret until the film's released.'

He laughed again and said, 'What were you saying about Frederick, Madam?'

She did not reply. She put four slices of bacon and two eggs on a plate and placed it before him. She got out the loaf of bread, dumped it on the table, and shoved it towards him. She said, 'You make me sick.'

He said, 'Why?'

She laughed, then.

He put his knife, bacon-smeared, down on her script. She grabbed it up, and saw it had left a grease-mark. 'Look what you've done!'

'It doesn't matter.'

That was true for practical purposes. It was the idea of her script having been smeared by Billy that mattered.

Billy ate as if he was hungry. She watched this with absent-minded distaste, for she was eager to have news of Frederick. She was angry with this man for being the only probable bearer of this knowledge, when all the world assumed that she had a charming husband, busy all day with his business, returning in the evening to take her out to brilliant gatherings and the opera, and hence to bed with her, the irresistible tiger.

Billy reached out for the bread and cut another slice to mop up his plate. 'I'm still hungry,' he said. She did not see what he meant by hunger, noticing only vaguely the crude manner of his eating. She brought out some fruit from a brown paper bag. He ate a banana, then another. He said, 'Suppose Frederick doesn't come home?'

That was what she always feared to suppose. There was a fear, too, that he would return. She could have prolonged for ever the lonely happiness of the early afternoon before Billy had arrived, with the baby sleeping on the floor, and nothing to do but wait for the furniture, feed and change the baby, bathe the baby, feed the baby, learn her part, and sleep till morning after morning. It was just the circumstances of things, and a failure of nerve, her public image and the film, that gave her this need for Frederick. She said loud and firm, as if to herself as well as Billy:

'I don't care if he wants to leave me. I only want to know.'

'Suppose,' said Billy, who had now made a thick apple sandwich, which he bit hugely into, 'that he throws himself out of a window?'

'What?'

'Commits suicide. I only say, suppose. He might throw himself out of a window.'

'Has he talked of that?'

'Yes.'

Frederick had said the same, and similar, to her many times. She had forgotten as soon as he had said it; she had simply forgotten, as one forgets a bad dream if one possibly can, and the dream does not always refuse to go away. Now she remembered Frederick's remarks:

'I might throw myself out of a window and finish with it.'

She had never replied. She had received the words with a nasty shock, then forgotten them.

She said, 'He couldn't mean it. They never do.'

'Don't they?' said Billy.

'Have you seen Frederick? What did he say? Where is he?'

'He said to tell you he'd be back tonight, about seven. Six to seven. Something like that.'

She gave him money and he departed, tramping through the long empty drawing-room. The baby lay awake on the pillow, following the man's legs with his eyes. As Annabel went with Billy to the door, she said, 'Have you got a key to this door?'

He said, 'Yes. Frederick lent me his, in case you weren't here. I was hungry.'

'I thought that was how you got in. Why didn't you get some money from him?'

'He hadn't any cash on him.'

When Billy had gone she put the chain on the door, and also bolted the inside bolt.

She washed up quickly, to get rid of the evidence of Billy's presence.

She filled the baby's bath and bathed him without answering his gurgles. Then she boiled his egg, two minutes, and fed him half of it. She prepared his milk food in the bottle and sat in the kitchen feeding him slowly. The baby looked happy and lost interest in the bottle when it was two-thirds finished. She laid him to sleep again on the pillow, pulled up the chair to watch him while he looked with surprise at a ribbon from his vest that his forefinger and thumb had contrived to lift. He started to squint at this ribbon, which presently dropped from his clutch, and his eyes closed in sleep. It was half-past six.

She had been reading her script for half an hour when the bell rang. She was sure it was Frederick. Her hair hung straight and straggly about her shoulders, in the fashion of that day, and she twitched it back from her face as she went to open the door. Three people stood there; no, four; there were a few others coming up the stairs.

They were recognisably part of Billy's set, whom she had met the other night, or if not Billy's set, another of the same kind. She waited for one to speak.

A girl said, 'Is this the party?' And behind her a thin woman with grey hair and a long black tight-fitting dress said, in Italian, 'Yes, this is the place, don't you recognise the little Tiger?' More people were echoing on the stone stairs, as they approached the main floor.

Annabel said to the group who now stood before her, ready to enter, 'No, it's not here. Do you want the Ketners' house?' The Ketners were an American family on the top floor, accessible from a lift at the back of the building to where Annabel was now pointing. She was sure this crowd must be bound for the Ketners, whom she knew slightly; the neighbours had said they gave many parties. Annabel was vaguely surprised that this particular set was among the Ketners' acquaintance, but she was busy pointing to the lift and explaining, above the babble of voices, that the Ketners were on the top floor.

But no, they had not come to the Ketners' house. They had come to hers. 'Frederick said seven o'clock. A house-warming party, Signora, your husband did tell us so – isn't he at home?'

'Oh, come in, come in,' said Annabel. She stood aside while they entered, about fifteen of them. More seemed to be coming upstairs. Annabel said to the woman in black, 'He must have meant it as a surprise for me. I'm afraid there's nothing in the house yet, no furniture really, only a few things for myself and the baby.' They were taking off their coats and pullovers and piling them in a corner of the hall. She was about to close the front door, and meanwhile was pulling herself together to do the thing graciously, but the woman in black said – 'No, wait – the others are coming up. They've got all the liquor in the car.'

Annabel left the woman at the door and went to catch up with those who had now discarded their coats and were moving towards the folding door, which stood open to the drawing-room. 'Please – quiet – don't wake the baby. He's asleep.' She switched on a table-lamp, for the light from the window was now dim.

The baby had wakened, but was not startled. He looked at her, made a chortle, and stared up at the painted ceiling, blue, pink and gold, chariots, horses and angels. A few of the visitors had come over to where he was lying, exclaiming with pleasure, pressing to see him closer, and inquiring his name and age. But another group was standing by the window, waiting for the party to begin, while some of them had gone to other parts of the flat. As Annabel took up the bundle of baby and pillow to bear it to a small bedroom out of the way, where she had arranged a temporary bed for herself, she could hear the sound of ice being broken in the kitchen, and voices, more voices, at the door.

They were making themselves at home.

As she carried her baby along a passage, she caught sight of the Eskimo young man who had been at that recent party from which she had broken free into the night; then she recognised a few other faces, and realised they were largely the same set.

When she had settled the baby she started looking about to see if Frederick had arrived. She said to one man, 'Did you see my husband? He'll be along soon. He must have been delayed.' He smiled and shrugged, and continued smiling, in a way that seemed uncontrollable. Assuming that he did not speak English she repeated the question in Italian, trying as best she could to make it sound not a question. These people must not be allowed to know that she had no idea where Frederick had been, or that she was waiting for his return with any anxiety. But the man continued smiling; it was a smile with the mouth only, and she saw him move a hand to his mouth to try to stop the smile and to readjust the facial muscles; she realised then that the man was rather ill.

She looked round to see how many others had come fresh from drug feast. The woman in black was looking for a wall-plug; she had in her hand a long piece of flex leading from an electric record-player that someone had brought in. As she knelt to plug in the machine she looked up at Annabel and said, 'Your husband thought of everything.'

It was impossible to explain, afterwards, why she had not sent them all packing. She was not sure, herself, how it was that the whole event happened beyond her control.

'You should have telephoned to me,' Luigi said, later. 'I would have come and got rid of them.'

'You were in the country, weren't you?' she said. On Friday evenings Luigi usually went to his married life in the country not far from Rome.

He said, 'You could have telephoned to the country for me. Everyone else does. My wife's one of your fans.'

'It was a nightmare,' she said, although she knew that it was worse than a nightmare, because it had been a reality, with a worse and heavier reality to follow and finish off the night with a thud on the floor of her mind. She said, 'I had to keep up an appearance of politeness, I just couldn't lose my head.'

She was confused, now, about certain details. When they started to dance, she noticed, wriggling among the younger and gawkier of the all-screaming visitors, a woman of middle-age, very like the other one in black who had arrived first at the door, except that this woman had thin, short-cut grey hair, and her lined face was without make-up. Annabel could never be quite sure, afterwards, if this woman, incongruously snaking her body with the young, had been real or imagined. Because, the frightful thing about her which nobody else seemed particularly to notice, was her dress. This

42

was one of those few years when cut-away dresses had been fashionable, the cut-outs usually occurring round the midriff or at the sides of the dress from the under-arm to the waist, exposing the bare skin. The woman whom Annabel saw, or thought she saw, had a skinny, blurred, grey dress with a diamond-shaped cut-out in the front of the dress stretching from her waistline to her thighs; in fact it was obscene.

Annabel's head was spinning, but, by will-power and the practised habits of her profession, she made it stop spinning. She went to look at Carl on his pillow in the little room. He slept soundly with one fist raised on the pillow by his head, as in some comic salute. Next she went to the kitchen, which was crowded with men. She was looking for a tall young American girl whom she had seen arriving, and whom she felt she could talk lucidly to. She wanted lucid information, and also she wanted to get rid of the people as quickly and finally as her public image would permit. She knew by experience how dangerous these people could be, later, with their tongues and their published confession of an orgy at the Lady-Tiger's. The tall girl had apparently disappeared. The rows of bottles in the kitchen, which had been ordered by Frederick, were still plentiful, and she had sized up the hopeful facts that the habitual drug-eaters in the party were comparatively few, hence the remaining majority would be more inclined towards liquor; she was anxious for the liquor to disappear fast. It was now past eight o'clock. When the liquor went, the party would go, she reckoned.

As if to carry hospitality to another part of the flat, she grabbed from the kitchen table an unopened bottle of vodka, which she first hid in one of the built-in cupboards in the dressing-room behind what was to be her bedroom, and then in an edge of nerves about all possibilities of the evening, she suspected that any liquor at all in the house might eventually be smelt out when the kitchen supply ran short; and so she took it to the adjacent bathroom and poured it down the lavatory. She went back along the passage and looked at the baby again.

She disposed of four bottles of liquor in this way. The fourth time, it was expedient for her to slip into another of the flat's three bathrooms, and there she found the tall girl asleep and unawakable on the floor. She left her there, and, in fact, under the impact of the night, forgot about the girl, who was subsequently discovered, still unconscious, late the next afternoon, and taken away in an ambulance.

Between a change of records, Annabel found the woman in the long black dress, and said, 'Are you sure my husband said he'd be along soon? I'm rather worried. He should be here. I hope nothing's happened. Where did you see him?'

'No, Signora Annabella, he didn't say he would be coming soon. He said he would be here, only that. He said we should all come at seven.'

'Where did you see him?'

'Via Veneto, I think. I don't know really. I don't remember.' She smiled reproachfully, apologetically and conspiratorially, all in one, a composite smile that infuriated Annabel. She went to look at the baby. On the way, she heard a key in the lock. Frederick, it must be. She intended to hiss instructions at him to get rid of these tramps and queer louts at once, at once. But it was Billy O'Brien, using Frederick's key. He had brought a journalist with him, a lean blond German whom Annabel knew and somewhat feared. He supplied information to many vicious gossip–columnists, besides writing a sedate one of his own. Annabel had forgotten his name. Billy immediately introduced him as Kurt, and said, 'Where's Frederick?'

'Oh, Billy, I don't know. He's not here. He must have been held up somewhere. For God's sake help me to get rid of this crowd.'

44

'Don't you like the crowd? What have they done?' said Kurt, looking into the drawing-room, craning tall over other people's heads. 'They're having a good time.'

'I wasn't expecting them,' she said, 'that's all. You see, I have no nurse for my baby just now, and I have to look after him myself. And also, I have to learn my part for a new film. And then, you know, I don't as a rule entertain in this sort of way, I . . .' She trailed off when she realised that Kurt was looking at her with cynical intentness. She realised she had made too many excuses for wanting to get rid of the crowd. An old and famous actress had once given her the following advice: 'If you must make any excuse make one only. More than one sounds false. None at all is best. It's generally foolish to make excuses and give reasons. Never try to explain yourself to others, it leads to confusion. Avoid psychiatrists.' Annabel had stored up every word, but sometimes she forgot to apply them. Now she was led to flounder further among words and phrases that might possibly convey to the journalist an unshakeable poise as a hostess, a warm-hearted sympathy with the bedraggled rowdies who had already paved her floors with broken glass, and a welcome to himself. She said, in a last effort towards this end, 'I'm a little bit afraid of disturbing my neighbours – they're quite poor, some of them, and they go to bed early. What will you drink?'

He was already looking somewhere else, and Billy was putting a glass in his hand. He did not look to see who had done so, but merely clutched the glass and continued to peer among the dancers. He has seen that woman with the dress, thought Annabel. At my house. She looked around for the woman, but could not find her.

She went to look at the baby. He had turned in his sleep, and now moved with a little cry. She hushed him, and kept her hand lightly on the tucked-in bundle of bedclothes until he had settled back to sleep again. It was nearly nine o'clock. She would have to change and feed the baby at ten. A street lamp cast a dim night-light into the room, and now she saw that someone had been in there. There was a brandy-bottle lying on the floor between the baby and a chest-of-drawers. Annabel smelt it. It smelt only of brandy. But she was frightened now, lest some drug-addict should slip in to the room and perhaps harm the baby in her absence. She lay down on the narrow bed for about ten minutes, letting the noises of the night break over her. She thought, one by one, of the available friends she could summon for support, but there was none she could trust not to scandalise about the party afterwards. She imagined she would be intruding heavily if she telephoned to Luigi in the country. She longed for Golly Mackintosh, who was in Paris. Presently, she heard Billy calling her name. She did not go out to him immediately, but first telephoned to the doctor who had attended Frederick for influenza and the baby for a stomach upset during the last two months. His wife replied, in her warm German gutturals, 'Dr Tommasi is out on an urgent emergency, I'm sorry. There was an accident in the catacombs at St John's Basilica, and he was called away to the hospital more than an hour ago. He should be home soon, Mrs Christopher. You would like him to telephone when he returns?'

'No, it doesn't matter – well, yes, perhaps he could ring. I'm sorry to –'

'The baby is bad? Your husband? Yourself are not well?'

'No, it's all right. I only want some advice about something. It's nothing, really.'

'He will telephone to you. Be careful, you work too hard in your wonderful work, Mrs Christopher. I know it.'

*

In the end, it was Billy who got rid of them. He said he had seen Frederick at about six. Frederick had been suddenly in a hurry about some business he had to see to, but had told him about the party and said he would see him there. 'Don't worry,' Billy said. 'He's been held up, somewhere. He's got that new script to revise, you know, and the director lives somewhere way out in the suburbs. You know how they get talking.'

Out in the suburbs, she thought, with that dreary little tart. This has got to come to an end, she thought. I ought to be married to someone worth thinking about.

Billy managed to hide most of what was left to drink before he pulled out the plug of the record-player and spoke into the sudden silence. 'We've got to go,' he said. 'Come on, all go. Annabel's got to see to the baby.'

They were nearly all gone within the next fifteen minutes, and within half an hour all were gone except Billy, the journalist, a small, sober, wiry Italian girl who was diligently sticking by the journalist on the odds of some opportunity or other, and, although it hardly mattered, the forgotten girl on the bathroom floor who was sleeping off the handful of barbiturates she had taken, and who miraculously recovered consciousness the following evening in hospital.

Billy stood talking to Kurt the journalist, with the girl standing alertly by. The mess in the flat was now clearly visible. The mess was everywhere. The new wallpaper was no longer new. The baby was giving small shouts which were his normal preliminary to a wail. Annabel went to prepare his feed bottle, clearing a small space for herself in the kitchen. Someone had been abundantly sick in one of the sinks. She changed the baby while he howled anger, rage, and all other synonyms for these words, pausing only for breath and louder strength. Then she put the bottle to his mouth, and with a final grunt as if to bring the performance to an end artistically, he sucked and forgave. When he had been settled down to sleep again Annabel found the three still there. 'Can we send you in something to eat?' Billy said. 'We're going to get some dinner.'

'I'm not hungry, really.' She looked round. 'What a mess!'

'Thank you,' said Kurt the journalist, bowing goodbye.

Billy said, 'I'll come round in the morning and help you and Frederick to clean up the mess.'

'I can get someone in to help; one of the neighbours. They always offer to do jobs.'

'Don't trust them all,' said Kurt.

'Oh, they're very kind,' she said, as loftily as she would in any of her best parts.

The girl said a long, formal goodbye, as if she had been to a banquet.

Then they were gone. She switched out the hall light. She had turned away from the door for less than a second when the doorbell rang again. She was certain that this must be Frederick, and fury beset her. She did not go to the door immediately, but waited for a second ring. Instead, the door was opened by a key; it was Billy who had opened the door, not to return to the flat, but to let in some people who had appeared at the bend in the stairs just as he had left the flat with his friends. When he saw that they had stopped at Annabel's door, he had found fit simply to let them in. He called out, 'More visitors for you, Annabel.'

Oh God, she thought – No! She was almost ready then to let rip at Billy, at everyone; almost prepared to drop all restraint, and shout at them, vilify everyone, regardless of her public image, or any other sort of image. She said, 'Oh, good evening – I'm afraid everyone's left.' But her arm did not support the welcome by moving, either to take one of their hands or to switch on the hall light. Billy slipped away.

The new people entered, the man taking off a scarf which he had hardly needed in the first place. The woman closed the door behind them before Annabel could reach it.

Then she discerned whose was the large bulk in the unlit hall: Dr Tommasi's. Behind him came another tubby figure and a juvenile third. He had brought his wife and little girl at this late hour. She was suddenly bewildered and came toward them with puzzled politeness. 'How kind of you to come out. But I didn't mean you to do this.' She switched on the light.

The doctor was still clumsily unwinding his silk scarf; he was looking round for somewhere to hang it in a puzzled sort of way, as if he were distracted about something and imagined himself in some other house, or possibly at home, where some coat-rack stood in the hall. As he looked round, his wife put out her hand for the scarf. 'I didn't mean to bring him – you – out,' Annabel said to the wife, who looked back at her with pleading eyes.

'It's your husband,' said the doctor.

'Of course,' she said. 'He planned this party, did he ask you to come? – I'm afraid the others have all gone. Do come in. Frederick isn't here, I'm afraid. The place, you see, is a terrible mess. What will you drink?'

'I take the child,' the doctor's wife said. 'Where is the toilet, please, dear Mrs Christopher?'

The child looked too large to be so escorted, but she took her mother's hand and Annabel indicated the bathroom leading off her bedroom. 'I don't think any of our guests got in there. I'm afraid the rest of the house is a mess. They were rather a bohemian set.'

She found Dr Tommasi standing in the drawing-room, looking at the floor, yet not looking at it. He said, 'We had to bring our daughter, as we had no one to leave her with.'

'Oh, that's fine,' she said. 'What will –'

'I speak of Frederick, now,' he said. 'Your husband –'

'Where did you see him? He hasn't been near me for days and I expected him tonight. He sent along a crowd of people, awful people, but he didn't turn up himself. Naturally, I didn't want any of them to know I hadn't seen him for so long. Where is he?'

The man's hand was on her arm, at first, it seemed, as if to steady himself, but then he seemed to want to steady Annabel.

'He fell to the ground,' he said. 'I have told the police that I would come here first, so that you have a friend, and my wife would come.'

'What are you saying?'

The doctor said, 'He fell to the ground. It was too late when I got there. I could see it was too late. Another doctor was before me, already it was too late, that was the doctor with the ambulance. Already it was there outside; but they had to get him up, it was difficult at that place. They found my address in his book, and they telephoned to me also while the ambulance was coming. They have tried everything, but it was too late.'

'What are you saying, "too late"? Is he dead?' said Annabel. She was trying to get one real fact from the man; one state-ment, so that she could start to listen to him. 'Oh, he didn't jump out of a window, did he? Is he dead? What happened?'

'I got there, but it was too late.' His arm drew her to the one chair in the room, and forced her to sit on it.

She noticed that the doctor's wife had come in. The child was absent.

'Where is she?' Annabel said.

'Gelda is all right; you don't worry.'

'Don't let her wake the baby.'

'She looks from the window at the floodlights.'

'Is he dead?' said Annabel.

The wife nodded. But was it a nod to signify 'yes'? Annabel said, 'Is he dead?'

'He was taken in the ambulance. You must come to the hospital now, please, to identify him. They have his friend, there, Mr O'Brien, whose telephone was in his book.'

The wife had brought her something to drink. 'I will remain with the baby,' she said. 'You go.'

Annabel tried to grasp some idea of a tall building with the window. A tall building, in the suburbs, in a little flat, that girl . . . She said, 'How did he fall out of the window? Was it high?'

He said, 'It was not a window. It was from the planks where the men are working above the caves under the Church of St John and St Paul. He was in the church when they closed the doors, they have said. They thought he had gone home. Then the men working still in the excavations have seen him climb over the planks to the edge of the shaft, and they have shouted to him, but it was too late. He jumped from there to the foundations where they have placed the martyrdom of St Paul.'

She said, 'Is he dead?' thinking of that profound pit. They had stood on the edge of the staircase that had been built for visitors to the church. It had made her dizzy to see so many levels of winding passageways, layer upon layer. Later, they had gone down by the stairs, part of the way, and traversed some of the excavated planes of the old houses and pagan temples that lay ruggedly within the intestines of the excavation. There, by tradition, was the house where two Roman officers had lived, converts to Christianity. This was the place of their martyrdom. Carved stone plaques in the wall had pointed the way. 'In these catacombs, these passages, their blood was spilt.' 'Here, they were brought . . .'

She could not as yet form the thought of Frederick dead, alone and dead. She thought, 'But why among the martyrs? Why?' She was trying to piece together what had led him there, since he was always led by something. She could not think of him as dead beyond questioning, later, on this point. 'Is he dead, though?' she said.

'At first, when I went down, he was living but not conscious. There was no hope. It was five, ten, minutes to reach him, down those difficult steps, right down.'

The doctor's wife said, 'It is sure that he died on the way to the hospital. You go, now. I telephone, now, and I say that you shall come. Maybe now already they send to the door the police.'

'Oh no, don't let there be a fuss. The papers will get hold of it.'

'They are there, at the hospital, the journals. They await you.'

Suddenly she seemed to gather her wits, and stood up. The doctor's wife put an arm around her. 'Poor young woman,' she said.

But Annabel was eager to know one more thing. 'When did this happen? When did he jump?'

The doctor paused for exact thinking. Meanwhile Annabel changed her question. 'When did he fall?' she said.

'It must have been half-past seven. I was there before eight o'clock, and the ambulance was there, to get him up to the top, imagine how difficult. But it was too late.'

Then Annabel got ready to go, possessed by a furious horror at the abomination Frederick had brought down upon her. He had sent that party, that intolerable party, to be blood on her hands, blood on her public image . . . 'Frederick said, come at seven, he'd be here at seven . . . a housewarming party . . . Don't shut the door, the boys are coming up with the liquor . . .'

She had looked at the baby, and was ready to go. The newspapers, headlines, the phrases . . . 'Frederick Christopher dies while Annabel gives orgy at her apartment . . .' 'Frederick Christopher leaves wild party to die with martyrs.' 'The Tiger Lady was Too Much for Frederick.' She thought of telephoning to Luigi's press secretary, Francesca. Then she thought better of it. Francesca was always interested in Frederick; she might be moved to turn tiger herself now.

A few months later Annabel was able to think, sometimes, of his death. And then, sometimes, she thought of it with pity and bewilderment for, after all these years, it seemed to her there had been a vast unknown about Frederick, now dead, alone and dead. In fact, she had never explored very far. Sometimes, after his death, it was possible for her to think of his death apart from its relation to the effect of his death upon herself; but not always.

4

She went to identify the body and give answers to questions, numbly overwhelmed by his unspeakable trick. The face was bandaged and decent. They had arranged flowers around the high trolley on which it lay. She looked and said formally, 'Yes, that is my husband.' She touched the forehead and kissed it.

The doctor had brought her in by a side door, to avoid the newspapermen and the cameras that had collected on the steps of the front entrance. On leaving, they found the side door was posted with a waiting crowd. The doctor went alone, to get his car, while Annabel was diverted to an even more obscure exit, a back door, through a long gallery, through a stone-vaulted passage that connected one building from another. The doctor and nurses who escorted her began to speak rapidly, consoling her, all in Italian, one after another, and so much that she thought they were trying to probe her feelings. Then she saw that they were passing through a big room where trolleys were being wheeled through side doors which swung open momentarily to reveal a descending ramp; Annabel realised that they were passing through some kind of morgue, or at least a central depot where bodies were being taken to await funeral arrangements, possibly in some refrigerator-vault, and she assumed, then, that the voluble escorts were trying to distract her attention from this fact. But now she saw that one of the nurses was weeping, and at last came round again to the con-clusion that these people were trying to console her.

She responded then, and did it well, and was genuinely glad to cry; and then was driven home through the inter-twining dark-lit streets, under the high-flying white flags of washing that swayed from window to window of the old palaces. The poisoner behind the black window-square, a man flattened against a wall with the daggers ready . . . she wondered how the film would end, and although she wanted to leave the cinema and go home, she wanted first to see the end. They drove round a deserted piazza with a fountain playing heartlessly, its bowl upheld by a group of young boys, which was built by the political assassin to placate his con-science; and past the palace of the cardinal who bore the sealed quiet of the whole within his guilt; with that girl now binding his body with her long hair for fun; while he lay planning, with a cold mind, the actions of the morning which were to conceal the night's evil: calumny, calumny, a messen-ger here and there, many messengers, bearing whispers and hints, and assured, plausible, eye-witness accusations; narrow streets within narrower; along beside the fearful walls of the Cenci palace, in one of the lanes where she had run from the party, looking for a taxi. The camera swung round to the old ghetto. Fixed inventions of deeds not done, accu-sations, the determined blackening of character. The doctor at her side said, 'There are the news-people at your door, but I shall order them back. Stay in the car, and I'll park round the corner.'

She said, 'Wait a minute, I want to see it through to the end.'

He said, 'There is no need for you to see the press tonight. These men must have some idea what you've been through.'

Then he saw her clenched fists and looked at her face as it caught the street lights.

He said, 'I have to take you to a good hotel; you have a private suite and I bring the baby to you together with some medicine that you need for your sleep. I shall send a private nurse to you as soon as possible.'

He drove past her house with its waiting crowd, and stopped in another street nearby, where the lively late-night life of Rome was still flowing.

'No,' she said then. 'I don't want to stop here. I'll be recognised.' The sight of the crowd at her door, many of whom she had recognised as her neighbours, had restored her to practical thoughts, as yet not fully formed.

But she looked at her watch and said to the doctor, 'It's just past two. I must say something to the press now, or it will be too late for the morning papers. Things like this are easily misconstrued, and I don't want the whole world to get the wrong story.'

'But you must sleep?' He seemed to be confused by this unaccustomed point of view in a patient, and began to flounder with his doctor's orders.

'It's essential,' she said, when he again spoke hesitantly. 'You know, I have a public image to consider.'

He said, 'You are very brave,' confronted now with the mystery of another profession, and conscious of how a doctor is obliged to pull himself together when called upon, regardless of any personal stress he might be under.

'Oh, one gets used to it,' she said. 'It's a habit.'

He said, feeling for his puzzled words as he drove back to her door, 'It was only that I thought you looked really ill, in a state of collapse. The shock . . . It is quite amazing. You are quite a frail, small woman.'

These words gave her courage. She was ready to be seen as a frail, small, slip of a thing, with her neighbours around her.

She got out of the car as the door was yanked open by two or three news-men.

The cameras pressed in upon her, they flashed. The sightseers pushed and craned. She could not hear one of the questions in the noise that babbled from the wondering crowd, but she clutched the doctor's arm and shouted to him.

'Tell them to let me through and come back in half an hour. I'll talk to them, then. I have to go to see to my baby. Just half an hour.'

The doctor obediently made this heard, repeating it over and over, as he made way for her.

She got through to the door, and beyond into the courtyard. There, a smaller group of people had collected and were being shouted at by the gate-keeper, who, tousled and unbuttoned as one having been hastily brought from bed, was threatening to call the police to anyone who loitered on the inside of the door.

Annabel said to the doctor in audible Italian, 'I want my neighbours to come up to my flat with me. Everyone wants their neighbours at a time like this.'

She spoke in Italian, but an American voice sounded near her. She saw a reporter from an international news network standing by with his camera. He said, 'This must be a terrible moment for you, Annabel.'

For his benefit, and that of any of his countrymen who might be present, she repeated her demand in English.

'All my neighbours. I need my neighbours at a time like this.'

'Quite right,' said the neighbours, one after another. They bore her up the stairs, with vivid lamentations, some tears, many exclamations of pity, and with furtive adjustments of their urgently shoved-on clothes; men and women, and several children and babies who had been brought along on the principle that children should neither be left behind, ever, nor ever stopped-in for, followed the famous actress up the stairs.

The doctor's wife was amazed to open the door to so many people and children. She had swept up the broken glass in most of the rooms. The floors and walls, never again to be what they were before the party, looked now, at least, less wet. Firm and solid, she was ready with her child already dressed for the drive home, and had expected Annabel would want to be dropped off at her hotel with the baby.

She objected when her husband explained that they must stay there with Annabel till the press conference was over.

'Press conference! It is not civilised.' They followed Annabel into her bedroom where she had gone to see her sleeping Carl, leaving the company of neighbours in the large empty drawing-room to hush their own children. Annabel sat on the bed while the doctor and his wife continued their argument.

'But why?' said the woman, as if Annabel were not there. 'It's the middle of the night. Why these people? – and to let in the newspapers, the cameras, now, when she should be resting? What are you going to give her to sleep?'

'It's a matter of her profession. You know how it is with me – one has to continue, no matter –'

'You are different,' she said. 'A doctor is totally different. This is ridiculous, for an actress to think of the public when there is a private tragedy. You have to serve your patients, but she is not obliged in any way like that. It's unnatural for her to have a press conference at this moment.'

Annabel said, 'You must go home with your little girl, now. You've been wonderful. I want to stay here with my neighbours.'

The woman looked at her with the suspicion of one able and yet unable to enter another's mind.

'It is what Frederick would have wanted,' Annabel said. 'I know he would have wanted me to carry on with my career.' She was pleased at the sound of her words, and repeated them in her head. Then the lumpy, silent little girl, who was there, blinking, beside her mother, pulled at the blonde fringe of her hair and said, in Italian, 'If that's what he wanted why did he commit suicide and make a scandal for you?'

'Gelda! Gelda!' said the mother, alarmed with an element of anticipation, as well as of horror at the actual utterance; she obviously knew her daughter. 'You will stop, Gelda,' said the mother. 'You will say no more. You will be silent.'

The doctor left the little bedroom and went to the neighbours. He could be heard above their voices, organising the children into a room leading off the big one, where they could be seen by their parents but not impede the serious work afoot for Annabel.

Meanwhile Annabel sat on her bed and stared meaningfully at Gelda's mother. 'You'd better take her home,' Annabel said.

The child's face turned pudding again. She stumped three steps closer to her mother as if to protect herself from Annabel.

Annabel responded at once with a protective movement towards the baby on the bed. She lifted him carefully, hushing the small fretting noises of his disturbed sleep, and, holding him close against any further onslaught, started to leave the room.

'You're taking the baby in there?' said Mrs Tommasi, indicating the rumorous drawing-room. From beyond that, where the doctor had assembled the children, came subdued squeals and an occasional thud, and from the other side, at the front door, came an inexplicable sound as of furniture moving, accompanied by fast and whispered conversation; this came from certain of the husbands who had been sent to fetch in from their houses some chairs for the occasion.

Annabel, still holding her baby like a triumphant shield, looked again at the lumpy little girl with extreme distaste and said, 'It's time she was in bed. I think you must take her home right away.'

The doctor returned to the bedroom, then, with a glass of warmed-up wine and two aspirins obtained from the neighbours. Behind him were the leading neighbours, the Signora whose flat was huddled somewhere at the back of Annabel's, the grandmother of many who lived at the back of that, and the lawyer's widow from upstairs who always spoke her thoughts and comments into the distance, as if passing information to her dead husband. These three crowded into the little bedroom with sighs of awe at the sight of the baby in Annabel's arms.

Annabel started to weep over the baby, holding the glass awkwardly while she cradled the baby in one arm and secured him with the other elbow. She craned forward her head to sip the wine over the baby's body. The doctor put the aspirins half by half into her mouth and she washed them down with the warm wine and let her tears splash on to the side of the glass.

The widow said to the distance that it was a terrible thing to be left a widow with orphans. The other neighbours, encouraged to tears as copious as Annabel's, said many times how true this was.

Annabel had finished her drink and now she sniffed in an effort of control and led the way to the drawing-room. Behind her, she heard the child's voice again.

'The actresses can make themselves cry, they have to learn how to do it.'

Annabel turned with a horrified gasp on her cynical enemy; she had discerned an echo of Frederick's voice, for ever questioning her sincerity, taunting, so that she had come to defend her actions fiercely, troubled by all this probing into motives, as a cat, too often disturbed in its sleep, becomes fierce. She half-forgot that her tormentor was a child. She said, 'Get out, you beast!' while the father in the meantime cuffed the child on the head.

'Quite right,' said the neighbours, more in commendation of the doctor's action than Annabel's words.

The child wailed like a knifed victim and clung to her mother.

'Get out, go home, leave my house!' Annabel said wildly.

'She is overwrought by the tragedy,' the Italian widow told the distant air; and everyone agreed with her. It was not customary to order children, however naughty, out of one's house, or call them beasts as if they were adults.

Annabel pulled herself together and joined her agog supporters in the drawing-room, leaving the doctor and his wife in the first phase of a domestic row. Someone had taken their fat child by the hand and led her, consolingly, to join the other children. On the whole, these children were behaving well; they were awed and interested to be in the foreign lady's house on such a novel occasion, and for the most part were content to stand around in the connecting room, waiting for the next scene to transpire.

Annabel sat down on the chair left vacant for her. The neighbours, with their instinct for ceremony and spectacle, had ranged those chairs which they had brought from their own best rooms in two semi-circles which flanked the best chair of all; this was upholstered in red velvet, and its arms were antiquely carved. With equal instinct, Annabel sat on this best chair and adjusted the baby. The press would soon arrive. The men sat modestly regarding the floor with their hands on their knees, they had taken advantage of the furniture-fetching to brush their hair and shoes and to put on a respectable necktie or at least a white shirt.

Annabel's tears had dried up in her fit of anger with the doctor's child. She now glanced through the door at the assembled children and, seeing the girl among them, said quietly, 'I think that child should be taken home.'

'She is only tired, don't take notice; she's only a child.'

'If she's tired she should go home to bed.'

The grandmother, whose descendants were already so numerous as to have endowed her with wisdom beyond the arguments of logic, now decreed:

'Let her stay, the little girl. She's only tired out, so don't send her home to bed. Let her stay with the other children, poor little girl.'

'Yes, let her stay. She can be in the television picture, too.'

The doorbell rang, but it was only someone's son who had come home in the small hours to find the house empty and a note on the kitchen table directing him to the party. The mother and son rapidly exchanged greetings, reproaches, questions, counter-questions, explanations and tidings, all of which culminated in the mother formally presenting her son, Giorgio, to Annabel, with the explanation that her son did not normally come home at this hour, but he had not been out on pleasure, he had been delayed in discussion at the Club.

Giorgio bent over Annabel's hand with lowered lids, and murmured his condolences.

'My son,' said the mother, aside, with her strong dark face closing upon Annabel's ear, 'is extremely intelligent. He has been made discussion leader at the Men's Communist Club. Very intelligent, thank God.' She then ordered Giorgio to go back to their flat and fetch in a bottle of wine from the cupboard, to which end she took a key from her bag and handed it to him. Whereupon the discussion leader, who had been expressing to Annabel his admiration and pity regarding the sweet fatherless baby now settled to sleep in her arms, dabbed the corners of his eyes and went on his errand.

Annabel's eyes were brimming again, responding to his sympathy. At the door, he met with the press who had just arrived, and who surged past him without wasting words, and entered the big room. There they found Annabel suitably arranged, with her neighbours now suddenly silent, sitting and standing around her with folded hands, hands open as if in appeal for pity, hands crossed on breasts, hands at throat in the gesture of sudden disaster, hands in despair, holding the side of the head, and in every other spontaneous attitude of feeling by which they could convey to the newcomers their sense of plight and solidarity with the bereft woman, just as successfully as if the scene had been studied and rehearsed for weeks. It would have been very nearly impossible, and certainly very hazardous, for any member of the press to ask Annabel an awkward or hostile question at that gathering, or to probe very far into the delicacy of the hour. Annabel blinked away her eyes' moisture, swallowed visibly, looked down at the baby and sighed.

'How do you feel, Annabel?'

'Chilly. Cold.'

Giorgio was sent for a woollen shawl.

'Mrs Christopher, had you any idea your husband was going to do this?'

'Do what?' she said softly. 'It was an accident, you know.'

5

In the first dawn light Annabel lay in the small bedroom beside the sleeping baby and summed up, for herself, the probabilities that lay ahead.

The press conference had gone off fairly well. Not well, but fairly well, and, considering the hunted private lives of other actors of spectacular name, she felt that hers had been secured for the time being. It was the first news-break that counted most. Anything that could be turned into a scandal with the first news would be done now; it set the tone for the next few days, these being the most critical days for the survival of a public image under threat.

Two years before there had been a very young, newly celebrated, Belgian actress of Annabel's acquaintance, quaintly famous in every magazine for strict morals, absence of lovers, presence of chaperones, dresses which covered arms, throat and knees, and for a speech condemning birth control. She played the successive roles of Nurse Cavell and Joan of Arc. Her public image had been less skilfully handled than had Annabel's, lending itself to jokes and easy ruin. But still, she had seemed ripe for a star career before she was foolish enough to call the police on finding a student under her bed in the small hours of the morning. This girl had heard a noise under her bed, switched on the light, looked, and found the grinning student. He had done it for a bet, but that was not his story, and although it all blew over, this actress never regained her hold. Annabel reflected on this, when the neighbours had gone, following the departure of the press. She felt she had arranged things well in the emergency. Her stroke of good fortune for the evening was that Kurt, that blond, hostile journalist who had come to the party, was not present.

She felt cold with a coldness that nothing could warm. She lay on her bed with the baby beside her while the white slits of dawn formed up between the slats in the shutters. That doctor's child had come running in, moaning, among the news-men and the cameras, with a cut hand, the blood running on to her wrist and staining her horrible fawn dress. The mother had shrieked. The father had got busy with the cut hand, taking the child off to the bathroom to wash it, and demanding clean handkerchiefs from the people around. It was only a temporary divergence. Annabel had made a move to get up and concern herself, but the neighbours pinned her down. Little Carl in her arms started to cry. One of the neighbours took him, and then another, and soon the baby was joyfully responding to the company, being passed from hand to hand in the Roman popular fashion. Cameras were plucked like guitars and whirled like barrel organs. Meantime the doctor's child had managed to say, quite clearly, 'It was a bit of glass from your party that cut me, Mrs Annabel. Why did your friends break all the glasses and leave such a mess? Oh, my hand's all cut, all over – look, there's another place.'

A moving-picture camera was trained on her, held close to the photographer's eyes. 'Didn't your husband like your guests? Was that why he –' But the doctor had yanked her away, fussily followed by the mother. The respectful voices resumed their bereaved questioning, and she was hardly aware of the questioners, for so ordinary and harmless were the questions that it was these themselves that seemed to be speaking.

'And you don't know of any note, any letter that he left?'

'No, you see our things are still at the hotel. We only brought a few things over.'

'You saw him today?'

'Oh yes, but I'm afraid I'm rather confused at the moment . . . I'll have to take the baby to bed, I'm afraid. I will never believe it was suicide. Never.'

'You have no plans for the future? Your new film . . .'

'Oh, I haven't thought of that, of anything . . . It was a shock.'

The neighbours had supported her with interpolations about her courage and her grief, and with signs and signals of appeal and warning to the news-men. One or two of the younger, darker, more eager of the press-men – those from the European papers – had seemed disappointed, frowning and shrugging at each other to convey their frustration, but still they were deterred by the worthy scene, arranged as it was, with Annabel and infant in its midst, like some vast portrayal of a family and household by Holbein.

They had gone, and the daylight of Saturday was coming. The baby boy slept on by her side.

One reporter had said, 'You had a party here this evening?'

'No,' Annabel said, numbly, as if hardly taking in the question.

Another said, 'You cancelled the party, then, when you heard of the tragedy, Mrs Christopher?'

The cameras came close. 'What party? There was no party.'

The neighbours were silent, upholding that principle of appearance appropriate to an occasion which they called *bella figura*. They may have seemed too suddenly too silent, for the last question began to repeat itself from various heads, various lips, of the questioners: 'I heard that there was some sort of house-warming going on at the time of this tragedy . . .' 'What about the broken glass? – Didn't that small girl say . . . ?'

'Oh, it must be a rumour. These rumours come from nowhere. I don't know about glass. Maybe I broke a glass. I had a drink of something the doctor gave me when I . . . when I . . . heard . . . Of course, we might well have had some friends along, but as it happens we didn't . . . Mrs Tommasi was very kind and picked up the pieces of glass . . . I must have let it fall . . . I don't know . . . When I was taken to the hospital, you see, to identify . . .'

'Yes, of course, Mrs Christopher . . .' 'Yes . . .' 'Yes . . .' 'It must be terrible for you.'

As indeed it was terrible for her. Annabel lay on her sleepless bed now, thinking that Frederick would have to be warned not to speak of the party. It was important that for the next few days they should both be careful what they said. Anyone who claimed to have been at the party would be disbelieved if both she and Frederick denied it. Then she shivered with the fugitive knowledge reaching her stunned brain that Frederick was dead, and that soon, in the next few days, there would have to be found an explanation of his suicide, and that he, who was a necessary adjunct to all convincing explanations, had slunk off, as he was doing so much these days. She closed her eyes, thinking how vital it was that he should keep quiet about the party, and then of his treachery in timing it to coincide with his suicide.

Shortly after nine on the morning of Saturday Billy let himself in, with the newspapers. She sat up in bed, startled.

He said, 'The papers are all right, so far.'

'Go away. The neighbours will be coming in to see me. I don't want them to find you here.'

'Why?'

'They would talk. So far, everything's all right. Leave the papers. I've got to feed Carl, he's sleeping late, he's been up all night. I've been up all night, too. I'm going to feed him quick and then go straight back to the hotel. I can't stay here. You go.'

She had pulled her dressing-gown from the foot of the bed, and was getting up.

He said, 'You're in one of your states.'

'What do you expect me to be in?'

'Stay there. I'll mix the baby's food and I'll make you some coffee. If anyone comes to the door I'll go and let them in and tell them the truth.'

'What!'

'The truth. I'll just say I'm a friend of Frederick's come to see you. What's wrong with the truth?'

'Oh yes, well I suppose it's all right to say you're a friend of Frederick's.'

'So I was. How do you mix the baby's food? It seems a pity to wake him, though.'

When he came back he found her changing the baby, who meanwhile clutched and pulled her long wisps of hair. The first Italian newspapers were unfolded with the front pages before her, and she took in the headlines and paragraphs at the same time as she dressed the baby, and even while she let her head be pulled forward and sideways according as the baby tugged her hair, she managed to gather from the papers that she was so far blameless. She was quoted in every paper as saying 'I do not believe it was suicide,' or, 'I will never believe it was suicide,' or, 'Frederick was not the sort to commit suicide.' She remembered, then, that this was in fact what she had said at the news conference, over and over again, to the obvious approval of the neighbours, and was relieved that in the stress of the night's happenings she had not finally lost her head.

She said, 'It's the first batch of papers that counts. The others usually follow the same tone. It's the tone that matters.'

Billy took up one of the papers, and translated aloud, '"No matter what they say, nothing will convince me it was suicide," said Annabel, pale and . . .'

'It's true,' she said.

It was not till they got back to the untidy rooms at the hotel where the Christophers had been staying until the previous day, that Billy told her of the suicide notes.

The baby was asleep, now, in the cot once more provided by the hotel. It was the only object in the rooms that had been dismantled and moved out in her absence. Some of her bags were still here. They had been packed and locked, waiting to be brought over by Frederick.

She said, 'I thought I locked those cases.' On one of the bags the latch was unfastened. She went over and tried the other lock of the suitcase. It sprang open. The other suitcase was closed.

Billy said, 'They must have forgotten to lock it again.'

'Who? Who do you mean?'

'The police, I expect they've had a look round in case there was anything to find among his things. Drugs or a note, or some evidence.'

'What cheek! I'll report it to the Embassy. They –'

Billy said, 'You can't stop them. Suicide's a criminal offence. And sometimes people are driven to suicide by blackmail, or some sort of threat. They've got to know.'

'They didn't have a search warrant,' she said.

'No, well,' Billy said.

'What on earth could they find? Do you think he had any letters from that girl he was carrying on with?' She went to close the window, for the rain had started to pelt, and saw, under the awning of the café opposite, the people sitting at tables, lolling with espressos or ices, young men and girls, youngish like herself, with no troubles, it seemed to her, except the rain. A man looked across from a table, dark, with dark-rimmed glasses, and waved up to the hotel window where she stood. He smiled largely and whitely; he beckoned. She shut the window quickly, with a sort of despair because he had thought her an ordinary woman, free to come down and enjoy herself.

She started to look among Frederick's things scattered about in the other bedroom. Billy joined her.

'They found nothing,' he said. 'No letters, nothing like that.'

'How do you know? What about his manuscripts and stuff?'

'I got here first. I got all the papers I could find. Only his manuscripts weren't here, of course, he kept some at his girl's flat and some with me. I got all his suicide notes.'

Something in Annabel refused to hear the last sentence for about seven minutes, during which time the telephone rang. The hotel exchange had been told not to put through any calls to Annabel, but impressed by a call from Liechtenstein, the girl had thought it right to inquire if Annabel wanted to take it.

'No,' said Billy, who had lifted the receiver. 'No calls at all. Take messages. Who's calling from Liechtenstein?'

Annabel said, 'It's probably Golly. Tell her to come.'

'If it's a Miss or Mrs Golly Mackintosh, tell her to come here to Rome,' Billy said into the telephone. He had difficulty in conveying this message in Italian, and was about to spell Golly's name, when Annabel said, 'I'm going to scream and scream. I'm done.' There was a voice unlike her own in her throat as she spoke. 'He left no letters. There was no suicide.'

'Mrs Christopher is not well,' said Billy, 'she's sick and tired. Tell everyone that.'

6

'I am sick and tired of giving you money,' said Annabel, fishing into her handbag which lay on the counterpane. She was propped on pillows now, having woken from the dead sleep of arrested hysteria.

The bright daylight of Saturday had passed and a pink-gold light had arrived on the buildings outside the window. 'How long have I been asleep?'

A new doctor, summoned by Billy, had come, a young Italian intern from a hospital, innocent of what it was all about, but only anxious to perform his job, collect his fee, and be away to the country on his motor-bike for his one free Saturday afternoon in the month.

He had not recognised Annabel as anyone special, being evidently unacquainted with latest developments in the film business. He had assumed, from her general surroundings, that she was an actress, and assured Billy he had treated many American ladies for fatigue. Annabel, although slumped and staring, heard this mistake and managed to utter the anxious word 'English'. The young man, unaware that it involved his patient's calling, being the operative adjective to the designation Lady-Tiger, waved aside the distinction and went on to inquire of Billy her drug-taking habits, if any. Being satisfied that she suffered from fatigue only, he produced a syringe, and Annabel had given herself up to the sedative needle.

Now, with a temporary nurse, obtained, while she slept, to wheel out the baby and buxomly fuss with him in the next room, Annabel was propped and drowsily awake. She had slept for nearly four hours. Billy seemed not to have left the room, and it also seemed to Annabel that he had been waiting for her to wake up to ask her for money.

'What time is it?' she said.

'Ten past five. Do you want some tea?'

'Yes.'

He ordered tea on the telephone while she fumbled in her bag. She said, 'What do you want money for?'

He did not answer, and she left her bag gaping open, her hand drooping on the counterpane. Then he said, 'The main thing, Annabel, is that I've got Frederick's suicide notes. All of them.'

She looked alert, remembering that this was something she had to see to. Billy had been talking of suicide notes, she now remembered, before the doctor came.

Billy went over to a chair where he had draped his coat. He took a number of letters from the pocket. They had been opened. He came and sat on the bed, holding the letters in his red-freckled hands with some of his fingernails dark-rimmed; her eyes were on the letters and she saw that his hands were trembling.

'One of these,' he said, 'was delivered to me last night. I got it when I went back to my room just after I left you with the party at the flat. I took a taxi to the church right away but I was just too late. Then I came here and found the rest. Evidently he wanted the police to find them first or he would have sent them by hand, as he sent mine to me. Wouldn't he? But I got them first, Annabel, I came here, and I've got them.' He spoke curiously for Billy, almost as if he were nearly in tears, as if he, not she, were suffering from strain.

She said, reaching out her hand for the letters, 'What do they say? If it's that sort of money you want, Billy, I haven't got it on me. You'll have to wait and arrange it with my lawyer. Of course, we'll pay.'

He smiled, showing his gums. 'Poor woman,' he said, 'what did the man do to you, what did you do to him?'

She held out her hand, still. 'Let me see them, Billy.'

'They aren't for sale,' he said, holding them away from her grasp.

She began to shout. 'Maybe the photo-copies will be, one day. But let me see those letters. I want to see what he said and what he's done. And I want to know what he's trying to do.'

'There are no photo-copies,' he shouted back. 'Do you think I've had nothing else on my mind since last night but go running around with a dead man's deadly poison, getting them photographed – the letters photographed? Photographed.'

The maid with the tea knocked on the door. Billy let her in. Then he put the envelopes on the counterpane while he cleared a table and drew it up close to the bed. The maid waited with the tray, glancing every now and again at the figure of mythology from the picture-screens and picture-papers, lying in bed alive and ordinary, with her photograph and the latest story of her life in the newspaper on a chair not far away from her; a thin woman really, not so young, here in bed; and, existing only in another picture on the front page of a Rome evening newspaper which lay face upward on the far side of the counterpane at the Lady-Tiger's right hand, was her husband, Frederick Christopher: 'Actress repeats: "I will never believe it was suicide".'

Annabel's right hand moved the paper slightly aside, turning over the picture, as it might be she had not seen it, while at the same time she both moved herself further up in a sitting position against her pillows and let her left hand rest upon the four envelopes that Billy had laid on the bed. The contents were visible above the raggedly opened edges of the envelopes.

The maid said, 'The boy is waiting outside for the key.'

Billy went to the door and found a hotel boy waiting there. He seemed to want a key which someone had called for at the service door of the hotel. This turned out to be a woman obtained by one of Annabel's neighbours to clean her flat, and who, finding no one there, had been directed to the hotel. Annabel remembered, then, that in the course of the night one of her neighbours had promised to bring her poor sister-in-law to the flat at four in the afternoon to give the place a good clean.

Billy produced the key that he had got from Frederick and gave instructions that the woman was to return with the key for payment when her work was finished.

The maid and the boy were gone. Billy closed the door, opened the window on the shaded side of the room, came over to the tea-tray and said, 'I'll pour.'

Annabel said, 'Where is everybody? Why haven't they been in touch?'

'Everyone's been in touch. There's a pile of telegrams and phone messages downstairs. There's enough flowers to open a flower shop, they're all soaking in tubs in the laundry.'

'How do you know?'

'I saw to it all while you were asleep.' He poured tea over a slice of lemon in the cup.

She had the letters in her hand. 'Wire my lawyer. Tell him to come. I've got his home number in Berkshire.'

'He's already wired you. He'll be here tomorrow night or Monday morning. Stop being frightened.'

'It's frightening,' she said, 'when people start taking over. Why do you want to take over?'

'I'm a friend of the family,' he said. 'We once went to bed together. Go on, read the letters, you don't have to keep a calm face with me.'

'That was a long time ago. It was nothing.' She lifted the top envelope.

'I know it was nothing. If it was anything to me I wouldn't be an old friend of the family, would I?'

'Look,' she said, 'just because I go to bed with a man isn't to say I'm going to rub shoulders with him.'

'Read those letters. We've got to decide what to do at the inquest. Then I'll go. You'll have to give me some money, I haven't any left. I've paid the doctor and taxis and other things and I just need some cash.'

'The inquest? When's the inquest?'

She read,

Mamma – This is the last letter you will receive from me, your son . . .

She looked at the envelope, and then at Billy. 'It's addressed to me,' she said. 'Why does he write like that?'

'It isn't addressed to you. It's addressed to a Mrs W.A. Christopher,' Billy said. He leaned forward and, helping his talk with his freckled hands, he said, 'That's a letter that I think he intended the police to find; it would have been read at the inquest. They would all have been read at the inquest.'

'His mother died three or four years ago. Why does he write "Mamma"? He never called her "Mamma".'

'He was thinking of his public image.'

'No, he must be mad – you must be mad. His public image

was . . .' She continued reading, while Billy said, 'At the inquest first, then in the Italian press, and after that, the rest. No one would believe at first that she was dead, afterwards it would be too late.'

He stood up, excited and bitter, almost smiling, and snatched the letter from her hand. 'It's what they want to believe that counts.' Then he started to read it aloud, and as he did so she realised how carefully Frederick had built this letter, how very diligently, as if his career depended on it. Every week, every day sometimes, letters from sons to mammas appeared in the Italian papers – in letters from sons in prison, sons on trial, from students who had killed themselves in a nervous crisis, from sons who had seduced their neighbours' daughters, or run away with their wives, from priests who had got married in France. 'Mamma. It is I, your son who writes to you . . .'

Annabel sat up in bed, alert now, and no longer bewildered. She sat up to hear the rest, fully strained towards the professional nature of the enemy, desiring only to know the full extent and scope of his potential force.

The telephone rang at the same time as the nurse and baby were loudly demanding entrance, having returned from their walk. The nurse was clucking and exclaiming, before she was inside, how everyone in the Borghese gardens had admired the baby, all the mammas . . .

Having let them in, Billy made a dash for the telephone and was about to lift it when Annabel said, in a sharp, almost military, voice, 'Don't answer. Ignore it.' Then she turned to the nurse, who stood with the baby in her arms, waiting to hand him over to his mother and amazed to see Annabel now so much in control; pointing to the other room, Annabel said in the same tones – curiously incongruous with the Italian tongue – 'Go in there. Shut the door. Give Carl his bath.

Feed him. Then bring him back to me here in bed, please.'
The stunned nurse stood.

The telephone rang again. 'Don't touch it,' said Annabel like the spy-girl in the film. Then the nurse, somewhat recovered, and consoling the unconcerned baby for some supposed injury inflicted on him too, went as she had been bidden. Annabel, by way of putting herself in the right, called after her, 'We have to discuss the details of my husband's funeral. Please shut the door.'

Billy said, 'Hadn't I better ring down and see what they wanted?' He lifted the receiver as he spoke, and inquired why they had been ringing a few seconds ago. It appeared that the woman who had gone to clean Annabel's flat had met with some difficulty with a young lady, but she was coming straight over to the hotel to explain.

'Tell them,' said Annabel, 'not to worry us any more. Tell them at the desk to pay her and let her go and fight out her problem, whatever it is.'

Billy conveyed an elaborate version of these instructions to the hotel desk. Then he poured some tea and looked around for the letters.

Annabel had them under the bedclothes. She had been quick to conceal them on the entrance of the nurse. Now she brought them out again.

'We must talk softly,' she said. 'I don't want that woman to see anything, hear anything.'

'She doesn't understand English.'

'You never know what they understand. A word here and there, a piece of paper with a certain type of handwriting . . .' She looked at the four envelopes in her hand, with the one letter that she had not had time to shove back into its envelope, and said, 'His handwriting is normal, it's perfectly his normal hand. It isn't shaky or anything.'

'Yes, I noticed that.'

'He's dangerous,' she said, 'I didn't realise that he was dangerous.'

'He probably wrote them some time before he actually made up his mind,' Billy said. 'He kept talking of suicide, and I thought he might do it. But I didn't think he'd have it in him to leave these letters.'

'He's put the date on them, though.'

'He could have done that at the last.'

'At the last minute,' she said, with the exceptional emphasis of the fearful.

The nurse had gone off duty and the baby lay beside Annabel, waving his arms and giving sleepy shouts that sometimes ended in a yawn.

Annabel sat propped up with the letters. It was her third reading. Billy had a bottle of whisky, a jug of water and a bowl of ice beside him.

Mamma – This is the last letter you will receive from me, your son. You, who have always been a wonderful Mother to me, a true Mother – forgive me for what I am going to do. It is my only escape from an intolerable and abominable situation. Mamma, my wife is unfaithful to me, day and night. Since the birth of our son she has changed towards me entirely. Orgies – outrageous orgies of the most licentious nature are given in her honour, far into the night. Sometimes I have gone to persuade her to come home from these scenes of evil and horror, but she laughs at me and induces her friends to laugh, also. She has come home, many times, to our suite at this hotel where we are staying in Rome, drunk or drugged, at ten or eleven in the morning, accompanied by men of the lowest and most degrading type. The manager of the hotel has warned me that if this continues we will have to leave.

You know, Mamma, that our good reputation as a married couple is famous all over the world. This reputation is a living lie.

Little Carl is left in the hands of maids and nurses – anyone who happens to be around. What will become of him?

I leave this life, Mamma, knowing that even as I go to my death Annabel has organised a wild and horrible party in a new flat she has taken on for the purpose. She is drinking and dancing there at this very hour.

When you have read this letter, you will not blame me. I thank you, Mamma, for the wonderful things you have done for me. Pray for me. Would that all women were like you. Unworthy, I die with the Holy Martyrs in the hope of attaining Peace.

Your dying son,

FREDERICK

Annabel folded the letter and put it back into its envelope. She said, as if adding up a sum, 'His mother's dead. There haven't been any orgies that I've been to. The party at the flat last night was entirely Frederick's doing. I always look after the baby. The manager of the hotel hasn't complained at all about anything.' She looked at the baby by her side. He was now sleeping. 'But I'll have to prove it.'

'Yes,' Billy said.

She said, 'It would take some time to disprove all that about orgies. It would take some explaining, why he wrote it.'

'Oh, yes.'

She said, 'Next letter,' and took up the next. It was

addressed to herself. She read out, in a bored, humdrum voice:

Dear Annabel – When we were first married, poor, and in love, before we had risen to fame –

She halted and said, looking up at Billy, 'I like that, that "we".' But as she spoke Billy had jumped up from his chair, with his thick lips aghast and moving without speech. He was looking at one of the open windows.

It was a bulbous white shape, small and bobbing, illuminated somehow against the dusky sky, about one-third the size of the window, bobbing half in, half out, of the room; it had a head, body and legs, but no arms, like an embryo ghost.

Billy had sidled to a wall, and standing with his back to it he let out a high-pitched, womanish yell.

'You'll wake the baby!'

The baby woke and started to wail. Annabel took him up and held him. She had got a small shock, at first, on seeing the apparition, but she had quickly recognised the familiar toy balloons of Rome's night-life, grotesquely shaped and fixed with strings long enough to float them roof-high. The reflection from the pale illumination of a nearby monument had given a slight lustre to this white toy which still bobbed in the window. It was joined, presently, by a blue friend with a painted grin.

Billy stared, his hands pressed back against the wall behind him. He looked as if he was going to sag. The baby still wailed.

Annabel shouted, 'Billy, it's balloons; what's the matter with you?' She turned her attention to her son, and easing herself out of bed with him she carried the baby to the window to see the funny balloons. His noise tailed off as the dancing, floodlit creatures caught his attention. Annabel looked down. A couple of middle-aged tourist ladies waved gaily up, very pleased with their holiday and balloon life. Annabel took the baby's hand and waved it down to them.

Billy had stumbled off to the bathroom. When he came back he found Annabel still at the window, now batting at the balloons which hovered there. The baby, held between her right arm and hip, was completely absorbed in the sight.

Billy said, 'Nerves. I'm sorry. Sheer nervous reaction. I've had no sleep, none at all.'

She said, 'I'd better get back to bed. That injection was strong. I could fall asleep.'

Billy said, 'Aren't you going to finish reading the letters?'

'I suppose so. Do they vary?'

In the letter to herself Frederick accused her of mocking him with her orgies.

In the third letter, addressed to Billy, Frederick accused her of mocking him with orgies.

The fourth was addressed to Carl.

My Son, when you are old enough to understand, I want you to know . . .

'He's done it just like the journalists do when they want to cook up a scandal. I hear they even invent letters,' Annabel said sleepily. The baby was in his own cot, now, making a sing-song sleepy noise. She said, 'What's exactly an orgy? – Have you been to any?'

'Nerves, it was sleeplessness and strain,' Billy said.

Annabel said, 'Isn't there any message from Luigi Leopardi?'

'Who's he?'

'Who's he? You know who he is.'

Billy said, 'I'm feeling rotten. What do you want Leopardi for?'

She said, 'I want to speak to him. I don't like to ring him in the country; there's his family there, and all that. I want him to bring some money, too.'

Billy took up the receiver and inquired for messages from a Signor Leopardi. He looked sick, and his red gums showed as he spoke. He looked like a ginger-coloured, fugitive animal suffering from exhaustion and hunger. He was writing down Luigi's telephone number, and when that was finished he seemed to be detained by the operator while she put him through to someone else. Annabel heard him say, 'Are you sure?' Then he was speaking English, presumably with the head porter. Billy said, 'No!' Then he said, 'How awful!' Then Billy said, 'Well, she's in no condition to see the police just now. Who are they, are they plain-clothes men?' And he said, 'Are they carabinieri in uniform, or –?' After another pause in which a voluble and excited voice could be heard but not understood by Annabel, Billy said, 'I'll come down.'

'What's the matter?' said Annabel. But Billy had left the room with a bang. She got up, yawning, and looked at the piece of paper on which Billy had taken down Luigi Leopardi's number in the country. She lifted the receiver and asked the operator to put through a personal call to him. The girl said, 'Oh yes, this gentleman has telephoned many times to you.'

The question was, how did the girl found by the woman on a bathroom floor in Annabel's flat come to be left there in a dangerous condition? It was a subsidiary question how the girl had got there in the first place, and by Sunday morning she had already opened her eyes in hospital sufficiently to be questioned on this point, and to confess, with a sick grunt that she had gone there to take part in a 'sort of orgy'. She then said she had 'not had a glad-jab, it was pills'. She then said she was grateful, and fell asleep. They had already found the remainder of the pills in her bag and treated her accordingly.

But how had she come to be there? Luigi had not as yet asked Annabel this question. He was reading the letters.

It was ten o'clock on Sunday morning. The nurse had taken the baby to the roof terrace of the hotel where other nursemaids and young children were assembled – rather more than usual, since these nurses of all nationalities were anxious to hear whatever wisps of news might have trailed from Annabel's rooms. Those American, English and European papers which had reached Rome had already taken over Frederick's death from where the Italian scoop had begun. Photographs of Annabel leaving the hospital after identifying her dead husband, of Annabel hugging her baby son, surrounded by neighbours, and of Annabel in her most famous and recent Lady-Tiger film were prominent on the front pages, with the accompanying text headed with variations of 'Suicide? Impossible, Says Annabel.'

There were comparatively few pictures of Frederick himself, and this was a point which no one but Annabel seemed to notice, and she did so under the influence of having just encountered the full extent of his enmity; she noticed this general lack of emphasis on the actual dead husband with a kind of regret that he was not alive to suffer the fact. She noticed and said nothing. Luigi had arrived from the country at about half-past nine, and the nurse up on the terrace with Carl was spinning out a few stray lengths of yarn connected with events downstairs.

Annabel was up and dressed. She was pale. She sat limply in an armchair sipping coffee and ignoring the crusty rolls and small litter of jams and marmalades on her breakfast tray. Luigi went back to reading the letters. He, too, had a breakfast tray. He was eating mouthfuls of buttered roll and drinking gulps of coffee while also taking in the letters and the fact of their existence.

In her hand Annabel held that script she had been reading, *The Staircase*. She had been learning her part, a social secretary to an Ambassador's wife, the day before last in the new flat, when Billy had walked in. The mark of his buttery knife was on it. She had tucked it under her pillow after the invading party had arrived, and she had brought it to the hotel with her, carrying it wrapped in the baby's sleeping-bag together with the baby. She flicked it open and focused her mind upon the page. It was like coming home after being stuck for many hours in a traffic jam.

97. Daphne stops on staircase. She has seen Lamont cross the hall.
98. Camera pans from her to Lamont. As he reaches the library door, hand on knob, he turns, pauses. Upward glance.
99. Camera takes stairs up from hall slowly, one by one. Reach Daphne's feet, buckle shoes, which slowly descend.
100. As seen from landing on bend in staircase. Daphne descends. Lamont remains at library door. His hand has not moved.
101. Camera pans to top of staircase. Lady Sarah's feet, pointed toes, elaborate slippers. Slowly moves to face, eyes. She is dressed for dinner. Resolute, she descends.
102. Landing at bend in staircase. Lady Sarah halts.

LADY SARAH: Why, Miss Vance, have you finished already?

103. Daphne, below, still descending towards Lamont, who remains at library door, halts for a moment, hand on banister, when she hears Lady Sarah's voice. Then she turns with a pleading expression.

DAPHNE: Oh, yes, Lady Sarah, I was just slipping out to . . . to . . .

LAMONT: Sarah, you know, Miss Vance does have the right to some fresh air in the evening.

Luigi said, when he had seen the letters. 'Are there any more?'

'Billy says no,' she said.

'There are copies of these?'

'Billy says no.'

'You paid him for them?'

'No.'

'Then he must have copies. You'll have to pay him sooner or later.'

'Billy swears that he didn't get photo-copies made. He was furious with me when I wouldn't believe him. Maybe he's sorry for me.'

'Maybe what, Annabel?'

'Maybe he's sorry for me.'

Luigi then committed himself to agree to this possibility with a gesture of head-nodding sadness.

'Yes, he should be sorry for you,' Luigi said. 'He should be.'

Luigi was looking again at the last page of the last letter, the one addressed to Annabel. He read,

You are a beautiful shell, like something washed up on the sea-shore, a collector's item, perfectly formed, a pearly shell – but empty, devoid of the life it once held.

Annabel said, 'It's all an idea. He never looked at anything, much. I'm not all that beautiful and perfect, and all that empty, but it was an idea. Am I like a shell, do you think?'

Luigi looked at her with the expert intelligence which first perceived her possibilities in that scene at the fountain – a terrible film, not one of his own direction, but he had seen her, a fugitive governess in the part, hunted between the carved monsters and the great heroic figures of Bernini's fountain in the Piazza Navona, with the hot camera lamps on her and the young men and girls of the piazza looking on. He had noticed, not Annabel, but her recordable image, eyes that would change with the screen's texture, something sheerly given in the face, like a gift that could be exercised – he had seen this at first and second glance. Now, when he looked at her again he understood more lucidly what the quality was that had impressed him with a sense of what he could do with her. It was a limited, provincial look, the semi-detachment of daytime propriety that constrained a savage creature. Annabel, so ruthless about life, so squeamish about death! – 'I will never believe it was suicide, never.' – When Luigi had read this, he felt it would have been a very good line for one of her films, had Frederick Christopher only continued alive, to play his part in her public image. After all, that image was not so far from the truth, she was a lady-like, genteel sort of tiger; but still, indeed, a tiger. Luigi said to her, 'No, you're not an empty shell, no, of course not.'

'It's just one of his ideas,' she said. 'His ideas.'

She flicked through the script for comfort, noting the lines and directions.

She said, 'That girl – she'll be in tonight's news. I've told the police I don't know anything about her. She must have got into the flat, somehow. There were dozens of people in the flat – all night – the neighbours – a press conference, too – she must be still in a stupor, thinking she was at an orgy.'

'What was she doing there?'

'Frederick must have sent her. He probably gave her the drugs.'

'Well, don't worry, the girl's all right; it's a miracle, they say at the hospital. She took a handful of barbiturates. It was a suicide attempt. You can't keep it out of the news. But don't worry.' Luigi looked worried.

'Why? Why did she do that?'

'She's said she was in love with Frederick.'

This gave Annabel to let the script fall out of her hand on to the floor. She stopped slumping and stared at Luigi with her tawny eyes.

'No wonder Frederick was driven to suicide with all these women chasing him!' She spoke like the jab of a needle, and watched to see if her words had gone in. He seemed aware that she was trying to stick a pointed idea into his mind, rather in the manner of his press secretary, Francesca.

Then he saw that this was a potential line of defence.

Annabel said, 'The women drove him crazy. They were all chasing him. In the end he got mixed up, totally confused, and went over the edge . . . Probably he thought I was indulging in orgies . . .'

He said, 'Do you mean to say that at the inquest?'

He was admiring her thrift; he, who was truly in a position to discern a talent for acting, came to rate hers very high. Her talent, he thought, is a rich one. As in life, he thought, it is the very rich who understand thrift while the poor spend quickly on trifles. He gazed at her, half-smiling, glad that his wife, after all, was different from this. Annabel was considering his question about the inquest.

'It depends how it goes,' she said.

He thought then that she was able to hear what he had not intended to tell her just yet.

'You'll probably have to go away for a while. To Mexico, or to some nice place. Take the baby and rest.'

'No, I want to do the new film. What about the film?'

He said, 'The new movie won't do for you any more if this about the orgies takes on. It would be a joke, your playing this part of Daphne, I mean the renunciation scene. The renunciation, where you give up Lamont because he's a married man, and that end scene where he gets to the airport too late. The audience would start to laugh, it would be a joke if you have been an orgy woman in the papers. And if we cut the scenes about Daphne and Lamont discovering the dope-smugglers in the mountains and risking their lives to stop them ruining the young people we lose half the movie. And if we didn't cut it we have laughs. You know, Annabel, that type of movie is a mockery and a laugh if all this about the orgies was even a rumour for you. We have some Vatican money in this movie, I tell you confidentially. For you, the orgies would make a big rumour. These journals live on stories about the new stars, a new star is in a dangerous position for two years, three years. Always, a star has some danger, but the first two, three years, most danger.'

He took the manuscript from the floor where she had let it fall and flicked through it as if flicking through a bundle of banknotes, assessing, without precisely counting, their value.

He said, in his well-formed English with the American turn to the Italian accent: 'We'll have to get a new image for you. You'll have to play wild, mad girls when you come back from your vacation. We'll make different movies.'

She said, 'I've had other offers.'

He said, 'It's too soon for you to be talking that way. In two or three years' time you can talk of other offers, you can bargain other producers, other companies. You've only started. In America you're nowhere yet. You would have been, and still might be, in a few years' time, but . . .'

He was trying to reduce her value, as if he were bargaining with a bazaar merchant. She said, 'Why are you so sure this story about orgies will get about?' She spoke quickly, untying the belt of her dress and then tying it tighter.

He did not answer the question. Instead, he said, 'Your husband must have been insane. Lucidly insane. Was he jealous of me?'

'No,' she said. 'Why should he be jealous of you?'

He smiled and said, 'You are so honest.'

'How do I know,' she said, 'if he was jealous of you or not? He might have been. But he had no cause to be.'

'All right,' he said. 'You don't need to speak defiantly just because you think I show a little power over your career. I guess he was jealous of your career, anyhow.'

'He was jealous of the baby,' she said.

'Oh, no, never. It was your career. He had great envy and resentment of it.'

'No, it made him miserable, but he got used to it. Finally, it was the baby.'

'Why?'

'Why? – Ask him. No one would believe it, would they?'

Luigi was silent and forgot for a while to be a film man.

Annabel said, 'This afternoon at five I'm going to visit the girl in the hospital. What's her name? – Sandra somebody.'

'Danya Lutyens. The parents arrived today from the U.S.'

'Which part of the United States?' she said.

'I don't know. What does it matter which part?'

She was thinking of something else. 'I'll have to make arrangements for flowers to take to the hospital. I'll have to put my black things on and go and see her. Why did she say she was at an orgy?'

'She must have thought she was.'

'Frederick probably told her to meet him there, at an orgy, an orgy. He must have done. He could easily have emphasised the word "orgy".'

'Now you're making a movie script of it in your mind, Annabel. Frederick was ill. You should forgive him. Try to forgive, tell yourself that you forgive him.'

'That's my business,' she said, 'forgiving him. If you're going to forgive someone even when they're alive the worst thing you could say to them, somehow, is "I forgive you". It means you want that revenge of letting them know that you're superior. And it's the same when a person's dead – now Frederick's dead with all this hell in his death – if I tell myself "I forgive him" I'll never forgive him really. The best thing is to just go on as usual from where he jumped off – that's forgiving, really. You just pick up the pieces and get on with it.'

'When I was a child we were taught to say "I forgive you" when one had done wrong to us,' Luigi said. 'Everyone was pleased to be forgiven by word of mouth. We used to say "I will pray to God to forgive your sins".'

'Well, it's different with us. To say "I forgive you" is an insult. And to pray to God to forgive people isn't very nice, either, let alone telling anyone that you're going to pray for them. It's putting on airs.'

Luigi said, 'We would ask our brothers and sisters to forgive us. Our mother made us do it. We were used to it.'

'I know a girl who was brought up like that, in England,' Annabel said. 'She was left some money, and she put it into an industrial garments concern and lost it all within six weeks. All the rest of the family lost all their money sooner or later. I don't know how it was, but that family was awfully rich to start with, and they ended up penniless.'

'Because of saying "I forgive you" when they were young? Is it true?' Luigi was eager for her words to go on and on.

'Oh, I don't know. They don't go to church any more. The father died, and the mother gave up the church on Sundays and all that. I've got a new nurse for Carl arriving from England tomorrow morning. I wish she was here now. She could even arrange everything, like my visit to the hospital and the flowers. I know she would. You'll have to get hold of Francesca for me, and talk to her. She isn't very sympathetic, which is hard on me. I think she preferred Frederick.'

Luigi brought himself to his senses now that Annabel had stopped talking about things not at hand.

He got up, then sat down again. He said, 'Annabel, the nurse wired yesterday that she has decided not to come. Possibly the idea of being involved in a scandal has put her off.'

'To hell with her. I'll get a secretary.'

'I'll talk to Francesca. She'll have to arrange anything you want. Annabel, your doctor's child told the police that she saw the girl lying on the bathroom floor in your apartment when she came with her parents to see you. She told them there was a lot of broken glass lying about and that the young lady was asleep on the bathroom floor among a lot of bottles.'

'Why didn't she tell us all at the time? We could have done something sooner. She's a beastly child. She's lying. This Sanya – Danya – couldn't have got in while I was there.'

'Wasn't there a party?'

'Yes, but I've denied it.'

'But you didn't see Danya?'

'I did actually. But I clean forgot her. I saw her during the party, when I was being sent frantic. She was lying on the floor, and she was there all night, obviously, but it clean went out of my head, of course, after the doctor and his wife and this frightful kid arrived.'

'They told you what had happened to Frederick then, did they?'

'The doctor told me what he had done. It wasn't something that happened to him. Suicide was something he did.'

'Well, it's the same thing.'

'No, it isn't.'

He perceived, then, that she was trying to pin-point her mind in every precise way, lest it should give way to turmoil. He said, 'It was only to be expected that you should forget the girl on the floor when you had this news of your husband, Annabel. Nobody would expect otherwise.'

'I went off with the doctor to identify him,' she said.

'I know,' he said. 'It's perfectly clear. But why are you calling the child a liar?'

'Because she's trying to prove something against me,' Annabel said. 'That child is a pig and a beast.'

'A pig is a beast, isn't it? You use the two words wrong.' He took her hand and said, 'You should go straight to the clinic and stay there for a week. Just come out for the inquest tomorrow if they insist. They only want to establish the cause of his death, that's all.'

'I shall deny that I ever saw the girl in my flat,' Annabel said. 'It's the simplest way. Deny everything. Deny that there were any letters left among Frederick's papers. Deny it was suicide – he was just dazed and fell – dazed with pursuing women. Deny any orgy. In fact, there wasn't a real orgy, anyway, only a riot and a mob. Have you had any news from that girl of Frederick's? Her name's Marina. Billy knows her full name and where she stays.'

'She seems to be keeping quiet.'

'She won't keep quiet for long.'

'How did you know?'

'Someone from the press will pay her something enormous for the story of her love affair. I hope they do. I'll stop this orgy story and put out one about Frederick being made crazy by women chasing him. They chased him over the scaffolding of the church.'

'Stop the orgy story? How do you stop the waves of the sea?'

'Have the papers got it? The evening papers?'

'There's that reporter, Kurt,' said Luigi. 'That tall man. He wants a story from the hospital and from the police from Danya. I think he's got it.'

'Francesca should have stopped them.'

'And I think,' Luigi said, 'that you'll have to just go away, Annabel.'

'And,' he said, trying to make some opening in her obsession, 'that you should then find a new public image, and –'

'No, I'm going to save my image. I've got my baby to think of. How could I become a wild woman in private life after being my sort of wife?'

'You should forget all that's happened. Just pick up the pieces and carry on, carry on, somewhere else, as you've said is the way to forgive. You should –'

'Get Francesca to arrange my visit to the hospital this afternoon. I would like a bunch of yellow roses that look as if they've come out of someone's garden, newly picked – not all got up by a florist. Not too big, so that I can carry them easily. Get hold of Billy – tell him to find some more girls who were in love with Frederick and tell Francesca to get a face-on photograph of that pig-child. I'll ring my doctor and see if he can't admit that his daughter's imagination was overwrought. If not, one of the neighbours will have to say that the child was highly-strung – *nervosa*. I'm not going to start any new public image. It's the widowed Lady-Tiger or nothing.'

'You don't have to be a wild woman actually,' Luigi said. 'Just be seen around at parties.'

'Orgies. To fit in with Frederick's story.'

'No, but if that becomes the picture, you have to work in with it, a little bit. After all, you like fun, don't you, Annabel? You would like some fun in your life, wouldn't you, and be photographed having fun?'

'No, I don't like fun, quite honestly. There was no harm in the story of my being a tiger-woman in bed with Frederick, because it was all supposed to be within our marriage. We were married, after all. But in fact, in fact, I don't like tiger-sex. I like to have my sexual life under the bedclothes, in the dark, on a Saturday night. With my nightdress on. I know it's kinky, but that's how I like it.'

'That's like my wife,' Luigi said to the ceiling, at which he was looking at the time. He sounded disheartened.

'And I don't like it upside down,' she said.

'Yes, yes,' said Luigi.

'And I won't live up to a bad name,' she said. 'Not for any movie career, I won't. It's the widowed Lady-Tiger whose husband was sent insane by other women chasing him – it's that or nothing. I then can marry again after a while. There's Carl. Open the door.' She ran, herself, to open it.

Luigi looked again at the script. 'It's possible we can start shooting,' he said. 'Possible.'

The nurse came struggling in, dragging the folded pram and with the baby in her other arm.

7

By Sunday morning, three nurses, besides the doctors, had already heard Danya Lutyens declare she had been in love with Annabel's dead husband. The hospital staff was all the more convinced, when they heard the new revelations, that other women had pursued and actually driven the Englishman, the husband of the famous marriage, to destruction.

Francesca had been located at Ostia and brought back to Rome before lunch. Her heart was not in the job of saving Annabel's image; nevertheless she put her mind to it. She briefed the Italian press, or rather passed information to them in the more tempting guise of rumour, before, at, and after, lunch; and now the news had spread throughout the hospital where reporters garrulously accosted everyone who came and went – nurses, doctors, domestics and visitors – putting to them questions loaded with information, in the hope of gaining new and even brighter facts and hazards. 'Did you see Danya? Is she still in love with Frederick Christopher? She knows he's dead? She realises? Has she spoken of the other women, her rivals, those that chased him in the Church of St Paul and St John? Yes, it's true, there were several women – three, four, I don't know – but one chased him over the scaffolding, he was trying to escape her. She was wearing a bikini. What is Danya saying? Does she know her parents are coming? Does she know Annabel's coming to see her? Grateful? She actually said she was grateful? Who to? The hospital? Italy? Did she say she was grateful to Annabel Christopher? And what else?'

Most of the reporters had dispersed for lunch at the time Danya's parents had arrived, straight from the airport, and the few who were left had to content themselves with quick photographs of the couple, accompanied by a young, brisk man who might have been an American consul. They were hurried into the building between a bodyguard of police who had only just arrived, having by now been alerted that a fuss was on outside the hospital.

More police had gathered and were standing around when Annabel arrived, at half-past three. The reporters and cameramen were back in full strength. A crowd of Sunday sightseers formed on the perimeter of news-men and police when Annabel's car drew up.

She placed back her black veil when she alit from the car. She carried a small bunch of yellow roses. She was unaccompanied.

'Why are you visiting Danya, Annabel? – Annabel, Mrs Christopher, did you know the girl before? – Did you know she was running after your husband? Was there anything between them? How are you bearing up, Mrs Christopher? – Can you tell us anything about the other girls? – Do you know their names? What about the orgy?'

She smiled slightly and looked at the patient policemen and the reporters pressing behind them, and, behind those, the crowd which was by now being augmented by others – young boys from neighbouring shops and women with their aprons, running across the street to join in. She had often been recognised in the street by passers-by, but she had never before drawn an actual street-crowd. She noticed that the press was predominantly Italian; Annabel did not forget to look up at the hospital windows; sure enough, most of them were occupied by peering and bobbing heads. She placed her sad smile up there, too. She looked around her, smiling as a bereaved mother upon her remaining children, and spoke in Italian with her rapid-syllabled accent.

'I am going to visit poor Danya,' she said, 'because I forgive her. The only orgy was the orgy of her own making. The other women . . .' She looked down at the flowers for a short space, then tossed up her head bravely. 'I forgive the other women. I forgive the one, also, who sent my husband to his death. My husband died the death of a martyr, in a church of martyrs. I forgive those who killed him.'

She covered her face with the flimsy veil. A sympathetic 'Ah-ah-ah' came from the women in the back rows. The cameras whined. She walked into the hospital where, two days before, she had been brought to identify Frederick's dead body.

'You were wonderful,' said Luigi afterwards, having seen the television shots on the evening programme.

But meantime Annabel had spent twenty minutes by Danya's bed.

'I'm grateful,' Danya had said weakly, with a puzzled smile, and closed her eyes.

The girl's mother, wan from the air voyage and anxiety, but still prettier and more slender than the dazed daughter in the hospital bed, turned with an effort of good grace to the nurse and said, 'She says she is grateful to you. And so are we. We are . . .' She realised that the nurse did not understand English. Annabel, in a black veil, standing before the bunch of yellow roses on the counterpane, translated.

The nurse explained to Annabel that the girl continuously said that she was grateful. Annabel duly translated this back to the mother, who said, of a sudden thought, 'Why, that's what her analyst told her to say at all times. She was under analysis back home, and I recall that she always said, "I'm grateful", when we asked her how she was feeling or how she was getting on in New York – that was when she left upstate and took an apartment – and she kept on saying "I'm grateful". It didn't sound right to us.'

The girl opened her eyes. A man of young middle-age, but with many lines on his face, was brought half-way into the room by a white-coated doctor. The man drooped, but this did not seem a permanent condition. He was the girl's father. He said to his wife, 'The doctor seems to think she's out of danger. A wonderful man. This is a wonderful place.' He took his daughter's hand and said, 'How are you, honey?' without really looking for any answer.

'I'm grateful,' she said.

But meantime he was being introduced to Annabel, to whom he apologised for his daughter's behaviour. Both parents were anxious to absolve themselves of their daughter's delinquency. They were decidedly keen to convey, on all sides, that the girl had been under analysis for a mental problem, and thus to lift the affair above charges of bad upbringing or any sort of blame. Annabel found this point of view reassuring. When she was asked, on her emergence, what the girl had said, Annabel replied, first in Italian and then in English,

'She said she was grateful. I am happy.'

Both parents conveyed assent, regarding Annabel with sympathetic respect; the father gently patted her shoulder.

Annabel refused further questions by dropping her veil over her face. The crowd, reminded that she was newly widowed, made a silence and stopped pressing. The reporters continued to edge in and out of the policemen's bulky figures, with questions and cameras; but Annabel made a sign to one of the policemen, whereupon three of them cleared a way for her to the edge of the pavement, where her car drew up. One of the policemen told her, in the course of this brief journey, that he liked the English very much, he had been a prisoner of war at Ackerly, near Blackburn. Annabel said she was glad to hear it and turned to hold out her hand to the girl's parents behind her, who had now been joined by their young blue-suited escort.

'We hope to see you again,' said the mother. 'Will you be staying in Rome for long?'

'I might go away after my husband's funeral tomorrow,' she said, 'with my baby.'

'Oh yes, of course. My dear . . .'

On her return to the hotel from the hospital, a young girl with shiny black cropped hair got into the lift with her. Between the first and the sixth floors, the girl said,

'Signora!'

Annabel looked at her. 'I'm Marina,' said the girl.

'Marina?'

'Your husband's friend. I've been trying to get to you, here at the desk, on the telephone – all ways. I couldn't write a letter because it was too personal.'

Annabel said, 'I don't think I can see you just now.' The lift stopped and the doors opened. 'I've got to attend to my baby.'

But the girl followed Annabel out of the lift, speaking quietly but not hurriedly, as if trying to still her own nerves. She was trying to open her bag as she walked by Annabel's side along the corridor, talking. Her hands were trembling. She said, 'He sent me a letter which I got the evening he died, that same evening. It is a terrible letter, such as no man should write of his wife, all against you, I don't understand it, and –'

'Come in,' said Annabel, 'and sit down.'

Annabel left her and went into the adjoining room. It was darkened by the slat-shutters. The baby was still deep in his afternoon sleep in his cot, and the nurse was sitting, steadily sewing in the very dim light as Italian women manage to do.

'I'll wake him in half-an-hour,' Annabel said. 'You go and get his things ironed. I've got some work to do with my secretary, so you needn't come back till six.'

The nurse, without stopping her sewing, said that the baby's things were already ironed, the girl in the hotel laundry had done them that morning. She plainly wanted to sit on and gather what she could from the person who had newly arrived but whom she could not see.

'Have you been to church? Shouldn't you go to the evening Mass?'

'There is no Mass till 6.30. If I come to bathe the baby, I don't go to church. It's no matter.'

Annabel was taking off her veil, carelessly, and said, just as carelessly, as she threw it on the bed, 'All right. Don't you need a light to sew by?'

'It will wake him.'

Annabel returned to the sitting-room, and quietly closed the intervening door.

She said, 'Do you speak English?'

'No,' said the girl, but she made a movement with her pretty eyes, towards the next room, to show that she understood that the nurse was very much there and very much disinclined to leave. She then swivelled her eyes upward to convey that life was like that. She had opened her bag. She handed Annabel the letter.

'If there are any bills,' said Annabel in a normal tone, 'my lawyer will attend to them. He'll be arriving first thing tomorrow morning. Sit down.'

'There's nothing owing here,' said the girl, rather too clearly, towards the next room.

'Oh, good. Don't speak so loud, Marina, you'll wake the baby. On the question of funeral expenses – my lawyer will see to those.' Annabel was reading the letter as she spoke.

And, as she turned to the next sheet, Marina replied, in a tone now modified to resemble that of the practised actress before her, 'I'll make a note of it. Do you know who will be arranging the funeral, Signora?'

'Mr O'Brien and Signor Leopardi have made all the arrangements. It will be at three in the afternoon. The inquest's at eleven. At Questura, you know.'

'Oh yes, of course. Will you need me there?'

'No,' said Annabel. 'Quite unnecessary. Let me see – what's all this about a party – of course I can't go to any party at a time like this. They must be out of their minds.'

'That's what I thought. They must be mad to write about parties to you like that.'

'They haven't read the newspapers, obviously. Even when my husband was alive I was always too busy with my films or my baby to go to parties, you know. A few – but not big ones.' Annabel was just then reading Frederick's complaint that she was always at 'nude orgies'. She said, 'I hate those parties at bathing pools where they all go around with hardly anything on.' Then Annabel waved and rustled the sheets of the letter: 'And this other letter here – did you take a copy?'

'No, did you want a copy?'

'It's not necessary, if I can keep this. My lawyer will tell you if he needs copies of anything. What about these other papers?' Annabel indicated the ash-tray on the table between them.

'They've been dealt with, Signora.'

'All right. Well, that's all. It was good of you to come on a Sunday.'

'It's nothing – at a time of your trouble . . .'

Annabel walked to the door that led to the corridor and opened it. 'You know where the lift is,' she said. 'Let me know if there's anything else. You can telephone me or Signor Leopardi. Goodbye.'

'Goodbye.' The girl looked unhappy, but was too afraid of the ear at the door between that room and the next, to venture any further words. She had turned to go, and the door had closed, but not clicked, behind her, when Annabel opened it again expertly, and said, following her out – 'Oh, there's one more thing –' Annabel had her by the arm and was propelling her along the corridor towards the lift – 'Just go along to my flat – you've got the keys haven't you and . . .' They continued along the corridor out of earshot and out of eyeshot.

'I never was at an orgy in my life,' Annabel said. The girl was suddenly voluble and excited. 'Forgive me,' she said to the Lady-Tiger. 'You must forgive me. I loved your husband, but now by this letter I see he was no good. I never went after him, Signora. Today, came to my house the reporter who wanted to know my love-story. He said many things, and asked was I in the church when Frederick was killed as he was chased by ladies? He said –'

'Sh-sh-sh!' Annabel gripped her arm and had her finger close to the button to call up the lift. So far, the corridors to right and left of the lift were deserted, but behind each door was an unknown factor. 'Keep quiet. It's all right,' Annabel said. The girl was crying, but she looked happier for the little bit of drama that had been her due.

'Who was the reporter? Speak softly.'

Marina spoke softly.

'I don't know the name. A tall man, fair. A German.'

'What did you say to him?'

'I told him I was never near the church. It's true. I said I was a friend of the family Mr and Mrs Christopher, to make dresses for the little boy.'

'You did right. Did you show him this letter?'

'No, oh no. He offered me money for all about the love-affair – nothing of this letter. Your husband must be mad. He never spoke to me of anything like this.'

'Do you think he was mad?'

'Yes. Sometimes I used to think so when he blamed life for his life.'

A door in the corridor opened. A middle-aged couple emerged, fussing with their evening clothes and discussing whether the temperature had dropped. The man pulled at the front of his coat and the woman moved a white woollen stole from one arm to another. They came to the lift.

'Are you going down?' said Annabel in Italian, pressing the button. Indeed they could not go up, since this was the last stage of the lift, but they did not point out this or anything else. They motioned and nodded amiably downward. They understood no Italian.

The lift arrived. 'You believe me, you forgive me?' said the girl. 'Goodbye, then,' said Annabel, pressing the girl into the lift after the couple. She nodded her head pleasantly to the lift in general and the lift doors closed.

By nightfall she had more or less caused the orgy story to abate. The baby was asleep. Annabel rested, waiting for Luigi, who was to come and dine with her. In the meantime she located Golly Mackintosh in Paris, and, partly to settle the general picture in her own mind for the inquest the next day, she practised her version of Frederick's death on Golly over the telephone.

'Finally,' said Annabel, 'he was actually chased in a church by these women. There were catacombs propped up by scaffolds, right down in the bowels of the earth. We were there together only the other day. Well, these girls were after him, one after the other. Finally one of them chased him right over the edge, right over. Then one of these girls crept into our new flat and attempted suicide because she was in love with him. My dear, I'm nearly ill.'

'What's all this,' said Golly, 'about an orgy at your place and the American girl taking drugs there, and the small girl coming across the body in a wardrobe?'

'A wardrobe? Is that in the Paris papers?'

'Yes.'

'Which paper? How could it have got into the French Sundays? The story only broke here today. What's the paper called?'

'I forget. I left it upstairs. I'm down in the lobby – Annabel?'

'Yes?'

'I'd cut and run if I were you.'

'Why?'

'Oh, I don't know. Come on here and join me, and we can both go someplace in Switzerland for a time. I know some people in Lausanne with a pool, they'd love you, you'd love them.'

'I don't want a pool. I went to visit the girl today. It was a terrible ordeal, but I came through it.'

'Which girl?'

'The American girl. Danya Lutyens. The one who took the pills in my bathroom.'

'Lutyens! – I think I know the parents, the family, if they're the ones from Nantucket. They have an apartment on 66th also. How do you spell the name?'

'I've no idea. They were at the hospital too.'

'What did she say?'

'She said she was grateful.'

'What? I can't hear. Who was grateful? The mother . . . ?'

'You were wonderful,' Luigi said, fresh from watching, on the television, her entrance and exit from the hospital. He said, 'The orgy story is killed. Everyone knows now that Frederick was pursued to his death by women. There will be no orgy story at the inquest. I saw Billy O'Brien this afternoon. He gave me the name and address of Frederick's Marina.'

'Marina,' said Annabel, 'must be left out of it.'

'Why? We don't have to say at the inquest that she chased him in the church. That can be implied. You only need mention her name. Billy will have to testify, as being the last of his friends to see him alive. He'll confirm that Marina was one of the girls. Leave the rest to the newspapers.'

'She's out of it,' Annabel said. 'I've done a deal with her.'

She produced from the depth of her bag a bundle of letters which Luigi recognised as those suicide notes of Frederick's.

He said, 'You still have them – you haven't destroyed them – you take them around in your purse?'

'They're safest there. If I left them anywhere else they could be found. Tomorrow, when the banks open, I'll get Tom to put them in a safe deposit for me.'

Tom was her lawyer from London. He was to arrive very early next morning.

'You might lose your purse. It could be snatched.'

'I can't go out,' she said, looking at the window from where, in the morning, could be seen the café with the free young people sitting outside – 'Even in normal times I'm noticed and watched. No one could snatch my bag.'

'You should burn them,' Luigi said. 'Burn those letters and wash the ashes down the wash-basin. That's the way to do it.'

'I think I want to keep them. Anyway, Tom should see them. You've seen them, Billy's seen them, and my lawyer should see them. There might be talk afterwards, and if Tom has got to deny anything, it's better that he knows what he's denying.'

'Talk – what do you mean? Do you mean I'd talk of this?'

'Oh no,' she said very politely. 'I mean Billy, of course. After a thing like this has blown over, there's always the temptation to tell the inside story to one's friends. Five, ten years later, I mean.'

'You are very distrustful, Annabel. How can you think of five and ten years ahead when you're in difficulties already for tomorrow – the inquest, the chance – who knows? – that your public image will be ruined – we might have over-looked something – how can you count the years ahead like this?'

'How jumpy you are! A moment ago you were saying the inquest would be all right, and nothing to worry about.'

'Well, maybe, yes. Don't look too many years ahead. Actors can't do this.'

'I've got my baby for years ahead.'

'You should burn those letters and forget it. Billy was good not to have them photographed. He told me himself, and in fact I believe him, that the thought never crossed his mind. I asked him very many times, carefully, about that. I was ashamed afterwards, of asking these questions. It was good of Billy to bring them to you without making some-thing for himself.'

'Good? What's good about not being bad?'

'You know the world. Billy is a good friend to you, Annabel. He has got Marina's address. He can mention her name in the courthouse. All the press will go to find her. She can't deny –'

'Wait, just wait a minute . . .' Annabel was taking one of the letters out of the bundle. She opened it. 'This is a new one,' she said.

She showed the letter to Luigi.

'Are you sure she had no copies made?'

'Oh yes. She probably doesn't know about photo-copies. She only knows there's a story about Frederick being chased in the church, and she says it wasn't her. Neither it was. It was nobody.'

'Did we say you'd keep her name out of it if she gave you the letter?'

'Not really. She gave me the letter because she thought Frederick was mad. I was interested in that. If she thinks he was mad, then others would, too.'

'Not immediately.'

'With all those letters – so many? Even if what he's written about me were true, only a madman would go on about it so much to so many people. It's a case-history in itself, this bundle of letters.'

Luigi thought for a moment. Then he said, 'I agree that madness would be the only ultimate conclusion –'

'And one of the letters to his mother, who's dead,' Annabel said.

'Well, of course, that could be a symbolic letter. The Italian papers would certainly have loved that letter. All the more so if the mother's dead. We like letters to mothers, dead or alive.' He leaned forward, frowned, and said, quite harshly, 'The immediate reaction to those letters would have finished your movie career. You couldn't do any more of these films with me. There would have to be some other kind of movie for you, later on; and then you are getting older – middle, late thirties, and you will take a part, maybe, in something not so special. And I'd have to find another star, make a new start, right away, next week, with that.' He was pointing to her film script, which was now on top of a chest-of-drawers beside the window.

She said, 'I'm hungry.'

'Don't be tempted,' he said.

'I won't eat bread, potatoes or spaghetti,' she said. 'Don't worry, I won't get too fat for the part.'

He said in a milder voice, 'I meant, don't be tempted to show off those letters in the courthouse.'

'Yes, I know that's what you meant. I want my dinner.'

'You should come out. Where would you like to go?'

'The nurse has left for the night. I don't want to leave the baby with anyone else.' She looked at her watch. 'Billy should be here soon,' she said. 'He can stay and have dinner with me up here, if you like, and we can get our story straight for tomorrow. There's only the doctor and Billy and me to give evidence.'

They were already eating when Billy arrived, two hours late. A round table had been wheeled in. There was a fuss of ordering Billy's dinner on the house telephone; the restaurant had closed, and he had to put up with cold veal when he had wanted steak.

He was extremely gentle. He drank some of their wine and ate several chunks of bread while he was waiting for his dinner to come up.

When he had been served and the waiter had gone, he listened as he ate to Annabel's instructions. Marina was not to be mentioned. Yes, he agreed. He wanted to see, and was shown, the letter. Somehow or other he got a butter mark on it. He said, 'That was very lucky that you got that letter. It's lucky she didn't use it herself in some way. It's worth a fortune to her. If we had cited her as a cause of Frederick's suicide, she could have produced it and sold it.' He seemed to fondle it.

'A reporter was after her for her story. I think it was your awful Kurt.'

'Did he see this letter?'

'No, oh no. I'm sure she was perfectly truthful about it all.'

'She hasn't had a photo-copy taken? – You sure?'

'I'm sure.'

'Well, you're lucky,' said Billy, folding and pushing the buttered letter into Annabel's hand rather roughly. 'That's all I can say – lucky.'

Luigi agreed she was lucky. He said, then, 'Could there be anyone else that Frederick wrote to?'

'Could be,' said Billy. 'But not likely. I know all the people he knew. Marina was the only one I suspected might have heard from him. She didn't tell *me* she had a letter from him.'

'Oh, did you go to see her?' Annabel said.

'No, but I got her on the phone. She was cagey and frightened. She said she didn't want anything to get her family into trouble. She said it would kill her mother if she had a scandal. She didn't say anything about this letter.'

'Well, we're lucky,' said Luigi irritably, as if bored with the discussion of their luckiness, and wanting to dismiss it. He went on to tell Annabel that his lawyer would be at the inquest to assist her, as a mere formality, but that there was very little for her to do or say, except that she did not believe her husband had committed suicide – 'Which you said already to the press,' said Luigi, 'and that is the right thing to say anyhow, always – And you say, now, that you believe your husband was pursued by so many women that he didn't know what he was doing.'

'Pass the wine, please,' said Billy.

'Stick to that,' said Luigi. 'If you are asked if you know who these women are, say you don't know them, and you forgive them. If they mention the American girl that took the pills in your flat, say you forgive her.' Then he said, 'I don't like this business of directing an inquest like a movie.'

Billy said, 'Leave it to me.'

'Only you don't have to forgive the girls,' said Luigi.

'No, I won't forgive them.'

'You only say you know there were a lot.'

'Really,' said Annabel, 'there's hardly any need for Tom to come tomorrow.'

'No need,' said Luigi. 'No need at all. He's not accepted in any kind of Italian court. My lawyer's all you need for the inquest. I'd have brought my lawyer along to introduce him to you, but he's been in the country all day. He'll see that you get good treatment and only a few minutes' questions. I'd put your lawyer off if I were you. Ring him now and put him off. We don't need him. The orgy story's dead. Definitely. If there had to be some quiet bargaining with the press, or even if Marina had wanted some money, that would be different. Put him off.' He was crumbling bread with his finger-tips.

Billy said, 'No, don't do that. Don't let her put him off. There are things to do for Annabel – all Frederick's papers and belongings. She needs her lawyer. Don't forget, Luigi, that she's been left like this, suddenly, with all her husband's affairs on her hands. You must remember she's only a woman. She isn't as tough as you think.'

Annabel gazed out through the open window at the stars.

8

Her lawyer appeared at the hotel at nine-thirty on Monday morning, and was shown up.

She said, 'Oh, Tom, you look very Italian, somehow, in these surroundings.' He did indeed look like a young Italian lawyer, lean, dark, shiny-haired, keen-eyed.

He said, 'Annabel – those letters that Frederick left – I can't believe how he could have done it to you. I've never heard of such a sinister –'

'What letters? How do you know about them?'

'A man met me at the airport – O'Brien. He said –'

'Billy!' she said.

'Yes, he said he was a friend of yours and Frederick's. I must say, I thought it was a rather tasteless way to style himself – friend!'

'He told you about the letters?'

'He showed me photo-copies – that was on the road from the airport. He actually had a car waiting – and this fellow came up to me just as I came out from the Customs and said, "Mr Escon!" – I said, "Yes?" – He said, "Annabel asked me to meet you. I've got a car here." Then he took my bag, you see. Anyway, I didn't really like the look of him, or his manner, or the car either – I mean the car was all right, a little English Austin, but the man didn't feel like your idea, somehow. So I said, "I think I'll take a taxi, thank you. I've got some papers to look at." And I took my bag out of his hand, and sent the porter for a taxi. Anyway, he wouldn't leave my side. I knew he wanted money, somehow – one gets the feel of these fellows. He said it was urgently in your interests for him to speak to me before the inquest. Well, I let him get into the taxi with me. He just left his car sitting there. Then he produced the letters.'

'How many?'

'Four.'

'He must have got them copied the night that Frederick died. He swore he hadn't. I thought he was sorry for me, really I did. He was so awfully kind. And last night he was here – terribly kind.'

'Well, you were deceived.'

'I know.'

'He suggested you didn't need to know about these copies. I told him that indeed you did. The letters might be forgeries, after all.'

'I've got the letters, the real ones,' she said. 'Frederick wrote them all right. One to me, one to Billy, one to his mother, who's dead, one to Carl. And he also wrote one to his mistress, Marina, but he never got hold of that; I did.' She had sat down to take in Tom's news. She looked rather ill.

'Tom,' she said, 'don't pay him anything. Not a penny.'

'You'll have to pay,' he said. 'I think you should. He says he'll produce them at the inquest if you don't. We've only got an hour.'

She started to cry, loudly, careless of the nurse next door who was getting the baby ready for his walk. Annabel screamed, 'How much does he want? How much?'

Tom Escon walked through the open door into the other room and took the baby from the nurse, tickling him till he chuckled.

Annabel came up behind him and said in a quieter voice, 'How much does he want? – The girl doesn't understand English.'

Tom took the baby to the window. The nurse was ready to wheel him out. She had been watchful of the scene. Now she murmured something sympathetic to Annabel, and added that the Signora would feel better once the funeral was over. Annabel pulled herself together and settled the baby in his pram. She waved him off.

'Children understand more than you think,' Tom said. 'You should be careful what you say in front of them, however young.'

'I know,' she said. 'It's like people who speak another language. That nurse-girl knows more than I think she does, probably.'

'Babies don't so much understand,' he said, 'as record noises. Then they sort of remember afterwards. At least, that's my theory. I'm always pretty careful with my two.'

She said, 'I won't buy the letters.'

'Well, look,' he said, 'I won't tell you how much he's asking just now while you're upset. But it's worth it. I talked to your man, Luigi Leopardi, last night on the phone. Of course, he didn't know then that those letters had been copied, but he did say they would ruin you in your profession however much we explained them away afterwards.'

She said, 'The price? How much?'

He said, 'A lot. A great lot. But you can afford it.'

She said, 'And other copies – what about other copies?'

He said, 'We could get a statement from him. He couldn't try it twice. He seems to know how to do this legally. They all do. Anyhow, Annabel, I agreed to pay him. I'm meeting him after the inquest. I was glad to have a shower after being in a taxi with him all the way from the airport.'

She said, 'I still can't believe it.'

'I'll have to arrange for you to sign some preliminary note

113

for the actual money. He wants it secured immediately after the inquest, or he'll hand out the letters to the press.'

'I see.'

Tom hugged and kissed her and told her to keep her chin up. She said, 'What time was it last night when you spoke to Luigi?'

'Oh, very late. After eleven. It must have been after midnight, Rome time. He said he'd just had dinner with you.'

'He isn't taking any chances. What did he say?'

'Oh, very business-like. He told me briefly about the possibility of scandal – he was very careful not to go into details on the phone – but what he wanted me to impress on you was that there was nothing doing for you in the film business unless you come out of this with the right public image. You've been built up on that, so you can fall down on that. It's brutal. I'm sorry you've got to face this horror. But it's only money, it's only money. We have to pay O'Brien under formality, as if for some kind of professional services. We're perfectly legal on our side.'

'Yes,' said Annabel, 'there were some special messages left among his papers. Four letters. I have them here.' She opened her bag and withdrew four letters. She had destroyed Marina's letter before she left for the courthouse. She looked across at Billy, only vaguely conscious of the hubbub that had started in the packed room with its wide windows open and the young green trees beyond. She had seen Billy when she was called to answer. She had looked across at him, and he had smiled and bowed with that little mockery of the successful practical joker who expects the victim to take it in good part. Now, with the deep voice of the magistrate beating above the hum of public sensation, she looked at him again. Even when she felt the letters being taken out of her hand, she looked at Billy as if anxious not to miss the least flicker of expression. He was staring at the letters as he had stared at the white balloon at her hotel window the night after Frederick died. Something was lacking, for he did not scream on this occasion; but it was the formation of the lips, and the stare, that she recognised.

The room was brought to silence by the magistrate. Annabel was asked where she had found the letters. She said, 'I don't know where they came from. They were just sent to me, opened, like that –'

'Are they in your husband's handwriting?'

'Yes, I think so,' she said.

Luigi's lawyer was talking rapidly to the magistrate, moving his hands volubly.

The magistrate told the court there would have to be an adjournment because of these unexpected exhibits.

She said, 'I wish to say there is no truth in what my husband accuses me of in those letters. He was insane.'

The magistrate said that was for him to decide, and the court adjourned.

She was at the airport, waiting for the plane to Greece.

'Why did you do that?' Tom had said when they were back in her room. 'It wasn't necessary,' he said.

She had the baby on her lap. She said, 'I want to be free like my baby. I hope he's recording this noise.'

In fact, she had felt, as she still felt, neither free nor unfree. She was not sure what those words meant. But she was entirely satisfied, now, to be waiting with the baby at the airport for a plane to Greece.

She had refused lunch and said she would rest. She had slipped away in the heat of the day, at two o'clock, when everyone was at lunch or had eaten lunch, and was about to rest for an hour or so. There were no police for her protection at the airport, no crowds. They were mostly at the courthouse waiting for her to appear again there at four o'clock. Her name had never been so well known. The funeral had been postponed as a result of the adjournment. A few people who had not heard this news on the wireless were surely at the Church of St John and St Paul already, expecting her to arrive there.

She had walked out into the street, at that lazy unwatchful hour, with a handbag full of baby things, a sling-bag over her shoulder with some of her own things, and the baby on her arm. Up the street and round the corner she had got a taxi. Nobody had expected her newly-televised face to appear at the airport among the crowds of tourists; she had gone unnoticed by the customs men, the emigration men and the airport officials. As she arrived, she had seen a group of people crossing from a newly-landed plane to the customs shed. She thought she saw Golly Mackintosh among them. But she did not wait, and was never to know whether this woman was Golly or whether she was not.

Annabel bought a third-class ticket, had her bags weighed, was helped by two cheerful students behind her to sling her bag on to her shoulder again, and now was waiting for the plane. Her flight number had been called. The stewardess came forward to help her with the baby, but she gave the girl her bags instead.

Waiting for the order to board, she felt both free and unfree. The heavy weight of the bags was gone; she felt as if she was still, curiously, pregnant with the baby, but not pregnant in fact. She was pale as a shell. She did not wear her dark glasses. Nobody recognised her as she stood, having moved the baby to rest on her hip, conscious also of the baby in a sense weightlessly and perpetually within her, as an empty shell contains, by its very structure, the echo and harking image of former and former seas.